# THE
## *hook*
### UP

A FIRST IMPRESSIONS
STORY

# THE
## *hook*
## UP

A FIRST IMPRESSIONS
STORY

# TAWNA
# FENSKE

Entangled Publishing, LLC
2614 South Timberline Road
Suite 109
Fort Collins, CO 80525
Visit our website at www.entangledpublishing.com.

Lovestruck is an imprint of Entangled Publishing, LLC.

Edited by Liz Pelletier
Cover design by Liz Pelletier
Cover art from iStock

Manufactured in the United States of America

First Edition July 2017

*Dedicated to my amazing street team, Fenske's Frisky Posse.
Thank you for being such incredible cheerleaders, sounding
boards, idea generators, laugh-makers, butt-patters, and
unpaid marketing experts. You ladies rock!*

# Chapter One

"Come on, you worm-slurping pile of—"

"Hey, Ty!"

Tyler Hendrix looked up from the handheld boom mike he'd been fighting with and saw Miriam Ashley, co-owner of First Impressions Branding & PR, in the doorway of his office. From her vantage point, she seemed unsurprised by Ty's colorful string of profanity.

He gave a respectful salute from behind his desk. "Hey, boss."

Miriam rolled her eyes and ambled into the room, her very pregnant belly preceding her by a good half-mile. "Are you planning to drop the 'boss' thing anytime soon?"

Ty grunted in response but set the mike down on his desk. She'd been his boss for more than six years. Even though Ty was now a partner in First Impressions and the head of their new offshoot video studio, he'd probably always see her as the one in charge.

"You're officially Speak Up's first guest of the day," he said as Miriam eased into the chair in front of his desk. "I'd offer you a drink, but all I have is lukewarm beer left over from the open house party."

"Tempting, but I'll pass," she said. "Actually, I just came by to remind you about my sister-in-law. You're renting her the conference space for some after-hours sales parties?"

"Right, yeah, of course." Ty said a silent thank you for the reminder. Setting up a brand new company in a brand new space had been hell on his schedule. What was the deal with the sister-in-law again? Tupperware parties or something. It didn't matter much to him, as long as she paid rent on time and left the room tidy afterward. He picked up the mike again and began wrenching on it. If the damn clip would just—

"I hope you don't mind, but I told her you'd give her a few tips," Miriam said.

"Sure," he muttered. "Don't buy boom mikes from discount photo supply websites."

"Tips about *business*," Miriam clarified. "I told her everything you've done to get this place up and running, and she was hoping to pick your brain a little."

"Sure, no prob." He stole a covert glance at his watch, trying to remember when his next client was due. An hour, maybe? God, he was so far behind on email and—

"I have to run, but nice job here." She started to heft herself out of the chair, and Ty jumped up to lend a hand. She waved him off and rested a hand on her belly. "Please. Even if I can't go more than ten minutes without peeing, I can still launch myself from a chair to run the universe."

"Peeing and running the universe sounds like the pinnacle of multi-tasking."

She grinned and ambled toward the door. "The place looks great, Ty. Nice work."

"Thanks." He tried to keep his voice even, but the compliment made his chest balloon with pride.

As she vanished out the door, he sat back down and booted

up his computer, toggling to the client management software. He scrolled until he found details on his first appointment of the day. L.E. Birmingham was the owner of a company called Pin Action. They manufactured custom bowling balls and other accessories for the avid bowler. Not really Ty's cup of tea, but he'd done his homework. The guy wanted a full multimedia plan, and Ty already had a spreadsheet full of ideas.

Footsteps in the hallway pulled his attention to the door. He looked up to see a stunning blonde wearing a red dress that hugged every luscious curve. She had legs that went on for miles and hair that slid over her shoulders like a golden curtain. Her eyes were the most mesmerizing shade of blue he'd ever seen, and when she smiled at him, Ty knocked the keyboard onto his lap.

"Are you Ty the video guy?" She gave a tense laugh. "Sorry. I didn't mean to make a poem out of your name. I'm a little nervous. I'm L.E."

*This* was L.E. Birmingham? Ty's voice had stopped working, so he bought himself some time by righting his keyboard and shoving the boom mike to the edge of his desk. That's what he'd tried for, anyway. He pushed too hard and the mike hit the floor, making them both jump.

Ty stood up. "You're L.E."

"In the flesh."

*Do not think about her flesh. Do not think about her flesh.*

"I'm so sorry," Ty said. "I wasn't expecting you quite yet."

Her cheeks pinkened, and she touched a hand to her chest. "Oh, no. It's my fault. I'm sorry. I emailed asking if I could swing by early, and I thought—"

"No, it's fine." He waved her into the room, annoyed with himself for coming off like a disorganized jackass. "Totally my fault," he said. "I've gotten a little behind on email, but it's fine. Come on in. Everything's fine."

*Jesus, Ty. Say "fine" one more time so she thinks you're a monosyllabic idiot.*

He cleared his throat and extended his hand. "Sorry, let me start again," he said. "I'm Ty. Welcome. It's great to meet you, L.E."

"Likewise," she said and took his hand.

Her grip was firm, but her palm warm and soft. Ty caught a whiff of something flowery and did a quick reshuffle in the part of his brain that expected the owner of a bowling ball company to smell like sweaty shoes and beer. Holy shit. He'd pictured a balding guy with a paunch, not a stunning blonde with eyes the color of the ocean.

*You are officially a presumptuous, sexist asshole,* he told himself. *There's one more trait you got from your old man.*

"Thanks for coming by, L.E.," Ty said when he finally gained control of his mouth. "Can I get you something to drink?"

"No, thank you. You're very kind, but if I start chugging water, I'll just have to pee, and then—" She grimaced. "Sorry. I don't usually talk about pee within seconds of meeting someone. Did I mention I'm nervous?"

Ty laughed, utterly charmed by her. It wasn't the first time he'd had a client confess shyness in the presence of so many video cameras, or even the first time in the last fifteen minutes that someone in his office had talked about peeing.

But it was the first time he'd felt so undone by a client.

"No need to be nervous," he assured her. "The cameras aren't on, and I promise I don't bite."

*Not unless you ask me to,* he thought, then wanted to kick himself again. *Get a hold of yourself, Hendrix.*

"Have a seat." He gestured to the chair Miriam had just vacated and tried not to stare at her legs as she settled herself and crossed one lush calf over the other.

L.E. rested her hands in her lap, glancing around the room. "This is a nice space. I hope you don't mind, but I peeked around a little. The restrooms, the conference room—all the décor in this place is amazing."

"That's all Miriam and Holly," he said. "The co-owners of First Impressions. I'm just here to run the new offshoot video studio and visual media lab."

"Speak Up, I know," she said. "I've heard all about it. It's an impressive endeavor, growing the business like that."

"It's a lot of work, but we're up to the task." Ty cleared his throat and commanded himself not to stare at her like some love-struck teenager. God, L.E. Birmingham would look terrific on camera. His brain was already whirling in a hundred new directions, thinking about video marketing strategies and whether she'd be game for being a public spokesperson for the Pin Action brand. What a great angle to add oomph to a fairly dull-sounding product line.

"Let's talk about your business," he said. "How long have you been running it?"

"Let's see…" Her brow furrowed, and she lifted a hand to sweep a few strands of golden hair behind one ear. "I started the company with just a small online presence when Henry was five. That's my son—he's six now and in first grade. Anyway, the company sort of took off several months ago, and sales have been going crazy."

"I heard about that," he said, ordering himself to stop having lewd thoughts about her. The woman was a mother, for crying out loud, which probably meant she was married. Even if she wasn't, Ty had a strict policy against dating single moms. No way in hell was he opening that can of worms.

Still, he dared a glance at her ring finger, surprised to see it bare.

*Focus on her face, jackass.*

Ty met her eyes again and cleared his throat. "You've got some impressive numbers."

"Thank you." Her expression was surprised and pleased

all at once. She settled against the back of her chair and relaxed. "I'm very passionate about the business," she added.

"I can see that." Ty did his best not to consider what else she might be passionate about. He was a professional, dammit. One who stayed the hell away from single mothers for their own damn good.

He rested his hands on the desk and did his best to focus on bowling balls. Not sea-blue eyes or mile-long legs or beautiful blondes who smelled like flowers. *Bowling balls.*

"Tell me more about the company," he said.

· · ·

Ellie Sanders crossed her legs and tried to focus on this business meeting instead of on the stupid-hot video guy with brawny arms and eyes so dark he must have ordered them from a catalog to match his jet-black hair. Her new dress itched like crazy, and she wasn't sure whether to play it cool or to dive in and talk about dildos.

Because that's what she needed to do. Her brother's wife had arranged for Ellie to rent the conference room for her after-hours parties, but she'd also urged Ellie to pick Ty's brain.

"He's one of the sharpest visual marketing experts I've worked with," Miriam had told her over dinner. "Super straightforward and no-bullshit, plus he's got tons of experience getting a new business up and running. You'll love him."

The fervor in Miriam's voice had made Ellie nervous. "You're positive he won't mind talking about a sex toy business with a total stranger?"

"Positive," Miriam had assured her. "The guy doesn't faze easily."

So here Ellie was, feeling more than a little awkward. It

was the first time in weeks she'd worn anything besides yoga pants, and it was clear she'd gone way overboard in her effort to dress like a professional. But at least she'd made it here, and Ty seemed willing to talk business strategy. She'd only planned to pop in and introduce herself, maybe check out of the space. Miriam must have asked him to give Ellie some special treatment.

Hottie video guy was talking again, so Ellie reminded herself to pay attention. And maybe to start thinking of him as Ty and not "hottie video guy."

"I had to admit I was taken aback when I visited your website," he said.

Ellie clutched the armrests on her chair. "You already visited my website?"

*God, please don't let him be a prude.*

She sat up straight and did her best to look like a smart, capable, professional woman and not a perv.

"It was very eye-opening," he said. "I had no idea there were so many different styles and colors and options available."

Ellie smiled and tried not to sag with relief. "We pride ourselves on having something for everyone," she said. "After all, no two people have the same tastes and preferences and turn-ons, so it's important to offer something to make everyone happy."

Was it her imagination, or did his eyes widen a little when she mentioned turn-ons? Maybe she should be playing this cool, not getting too explicit about any of Madam Butterfly's products.

"I see what you mean about being passionate about your products," he said. "I'm betting that really shines through to your customers."

"I hope so," she said. "I'm just getting started with the more face-to-face stuff, instead of just online marketing. To be honest, I wasn't sure that's the way to go."

"I can tell within five minutes of meeting you that you made the right call," he said. "The personal touch goes a long way in your business."

"That it does." Ellie smiled and tried to figure out if he was making a sex-toy joke or just being professional. Hello, awkward.

"I was impressed by some of the new products the company is rolling out," he said.

She nodded, amazed he'd done so much homework. Miriam wasn't kidding about how seriously he took his job. Ellie tried to think of something smart to say about Madame Butterfly's new offerings. Something Ty might relate to.

"The new Gentleman's Choice line will take some guys' game to a whole new level." Ugh. She wanted to kick herself. Would he take that as a come-on?

But Ty just smiled and folded his hands on the desk, and Ellie tried not to ogle his biceps. Or his forearms. Or his chest. Or—really, she should just study his pencil holder or something.

"I was noticing that new glow-in-the-dark line," he said. "There's some terrific visual marketing appeal there."

"That's a great point." Dammit, she should have brought a notepad or something to write this stuff down.

Ty picked up a letter opener and tapped it a few times on the edge of his desk before setting it down again. "If you're open to making a few videos, we could do some cool things in the studio with the glow-in-the-dark stuff. Maybe switch off the lights and have you hold one up and move it around a little. It's not too heavy for that, is it?"

Ellie laughed and shook her head. "No. It's definitely one of our biggest models, but I can handle it."

Ugh, did she sound too eager? He was right—the new Glow Bright Joy Stick vibrator was an awesome product, but no way in hell was she waving one around on camera. Showing it at a party was one thing, but video was different. Besides being camera shy, she didn't want to sit there in the carpool line wondering if the other moms had watched footage of her wielding a giant, glowing penis.

But if an average, slightly-exhausted single mom could embrace her sexuality and talk candidly about adult products, maybe she'd inspire other women to do the same.

"I guess I'm open to considering video," she said carefully. "Is there a way to, um…keep it subtle?"

"We'd play it however you like," Ty said, shoving his shirt-sleeves up and distracting Ellie with his arms again. "The important thing is for customers to actually see the products. I also think you'd get a lot of mileage out of how-to videos."

Ellie swallowed hard. This was not what she'd expected, but she wanted to keep an open mind. "What do you mean?"

"Maybe something where you showcase some of the different techniques. Like I was reading up on 'angle of entry' and how not everyone understands the importance of that."

"Oh. Right, yes, it's very important." Ellie forced herself not to frown. He was offering free advice, so it wasn't her place to shut him down. And he'd clearly done his homework if he knew about Madame Butterfly's line of g-spot vibrators angled for maximum pleasure. It was true plenty of women didn't know how that worked. Maybe an educational component would be helpful.

He was still talking, so Ellie told herself to listen instead of fretting about the prospect of starring in some trashy late-night cable TV infomercial. She could politely decline later, right?

"Reading about the angle of entry stuff was actually pretty fascinating," he continued, "I had no idea a four or five-degree shift can have such a huge impact on the strike pocket."

Strike pocket? Huh. Plenty of her customers used cutesie slang terms for their vaginas, but that was a new one on her. Ellie licked her lips. "It certainly makes a difference," she said. "The sensation is totally different when you have it just right."

Ty grinned and flattened his hands on the desk, and Ellie ordered herself not to stare at them. God, how long had it been since she'd been groped by anything that wasn't battery-powered? Much too long if she was breaking out in hives just sitting three feet from an attractive man.

"I was reading up on some of the other industry terminology," Ty continued, and Ellie snapped her gaze back to his face. "Have you ever thought about writing a few educational blog posts?"

"Blog posts?" Ellie folded her hands in her lap. "What did you have in mind?"

"Maybe something about whether you're a squeezer or a stroker and how that might impact your overall ball handling."

"Oh." Ellie flushed, surprised he'd gotten so graphic so quickly. Not that she was complaining. It was refreshing, honestly, to be around a man who was so candid about sexuality. "I hadn't thought about doing anything quite that specific. You think there'd be enough readers who'd find it interesting?"

"Definitely. Your customers are hungry for information. They're looking for something no one else is giving them, so there's no sense beating around the bush."

She gave an awkward little laugh, not sure if that was meant to be a naughty euphemism. She was so out of practice. Some men freaked when she talked about sex. Her brother pretended she sold Tupperware or candles or leggings, though Ellie knew her sister-in-law had introduced him to more than one Madame Butterfly product.

"I love the idea of approaching things from an educational angle," Ellie said. "Did you have any other suggestions?"

Ty leaned back a little in his chair, and Ellie could have sworn his eyes drop to her cleavage.

*Good,* her libido telegraphed. *Look all you like, hot stuff.*

Did women even call men "hot stuff" ?

"My father used to clean his balls constantly," Ty said.

The words splashed a little cool water on Ellie's libido, and she tried not to jerk in surprise.

"What about a tutorial on ball cleaning?" he continued. "Maybe talking about the importance of removing all the oils, making sure there's nothing stuck in any of the holes."

"Wow. Um, yes, I guess that is important." Her cheeks warmed as she processed the fact that he'd headed down this path. What the hell?

But he was the marketing expert and this was just brainstorming, right? Ellie cleared her throat. "Speaking of oils, did you see we're rolling out several new products in our Kneads and Desires Rubdown Line?"

Ty grinned, and something warm flipped over in Ellie's gut. "I love all the product names you guys have," he said. "The Heavy Hammer, the Big Hitter, the Perfect Pearl—"

"The Boom Boom Pow is my personal favorite," she said, laughing. "The name, I mean—I haven't actually tested all the products. There are so many, and they're adding new ones all the time. I can't keep track of all the names."

"I can imagine," he said. "Going back to the subject of cleaning, you guys have special products for that, right?"

"Definitely," Ellie said. "We've been trying to encourage everyone to buy a bottle of cleaner with every toy purchase."

"Toys," he repeated, his expression thoughtful. "I love that. Having a sense of playfulness about this is going to be key to making it a whole lot sexier. And sexy sells."

"So I've heard." She grinned and wondered if she was flirting. Is this what flirting looked like? She'd have to ask Miriam.

"What if you did some sort of giveaway?" he said. "Like maybe you write some copy about proper cleaning techniques, and then offer a free bottle of cleaner for every hundred dollars spent on new products?"

"That's brilliant!" Ellie grinned. "Any other ideas?"

Ty leaned back a little and splayed his fingers over the armrests of his chair. "Well, like I said, how-to videos are hot right now. What if you focused on something like how crucial it is to have your fingers measured? I read an article about why you need to be sure they fit properly in the holes."

"Oh." Ellie stared at Ty's fingers for a few beats then frowned. "Well, I don't think that's usually a problem, but I guess I'd have to read the article."

"Or there are a lot of other ways to come at it," he said. "Like maybe a whole series on proper hole drilling. It's quite the science, from what I've seen."

"Uh-huh," Ellie agreed. Her mouth had gone dry, and she wished now that she'd taken him up on the offer of water. "So you're thinking these posts would be targeted to both male and female customers?"

"Absolutely. Opening your market up to both genders can help diversify your offerings and reach an audience you haven't penetrated before."

"Huh." Crap. This was sounding way more explicit than she'd planned. Still, she wanted to hear him out. Ellie gave him a bright smile. "I appreciate the ideas."

"Definitely. I'm happy to help brainstorm." He leaned forward in his chair again, and Ellie dropped her gaze to his chest. God, the man was ripped. What would he look like with his shirt off?

"I need to do a little more research on this one, but what about something on PAP?" he suggested.

"That's a great idea," Ellie said, relieved to be off the video track. "Women's health is extremely important to the company. Maybe we could even do some sort of annual reminder."

Ty cocked his head. "I didn't realize that's something you need to check every year."

"Well, the American College of Obstetrics and Gynecology changed the recommendations to every three years, but a lot of gynecologists still suggest doing it annually to be safe."

"Wow." He looked befuddled. "I no idea the American College of Obstetrics and Gynecology weighed in on bowling."

Ellie blinked. There was a funny buzzing sound in the back of her brain, and it occurred to her there was something strange about this conversation. "Bowling?"

"I mean, I guess it makes sense," Ty continued, oblivious to Ellie's alarm. "From what I've read, knowing your Positive Access Point—your PAP, I mean—that's such a key part of understanding the axis your ball rolls on as it travels down the lane. I can see how getting it checked regularly can help prevent injury to—"

"Ty?"

"Yeah?"

Ellie gripped the armrests again. Her palms had started sweating, and her tongue turned to sandpaper against the roof of her mouth. "What are you talking about?"

Ty frowned. "I'm sorry, am I pronouncing it wrong? I guess I assumed it rhymed with snap, but maybe you spell it out as P-A-P or just—"

"We're not talking about Pap smears?"

"What?" He blinked, horror flashing across his face. "No! I'm so sorry if I offended you. I just thought—"

"You thought we were talking about...bowling?" Her brain did a slow rewind through the last ten minutes, replaying snippets of their conversation. "Oh, dear Lord."

"Is there a problem?" He frowned. "You are L.E. Birmingham, right? Owner of Pin Action Bowling Supplies?"

The ground shifted beneath her, and Ellie couldn't breathe. "I'm Ellie *Sanders*, owner of Madam Butterfly. We sell sexual aids and adult products and—"

"Oh, Jesus." Ty slid his hands down his face, which had gone unusually pale. He grabbed his laptop and started clicking keys, muttering softly under his breath.

*"Goddamn chode-stroking jackwad…"*

Ellie sat quietly, hands on her lap, while Ty produced the most creative string of expletives she'd ever heard. It made her feel better, knowing she wasn't the only one who'd talked dirty in this meeting. On purpose, anyway.

When Ty met her eyes again, his expression was grave. "You're Miriam's sister-in-law," he said slowly. "And you emailed me about coming in today."

She nodded, not sure how their wires had gotten crossed. "That's right."

His throat moved as he swallowed hard. "I'm so very sorry, Mrs. Sanders."

"Ms.," she said without thinking. "Ms. Sanders. I'm not married. But you can call me Ellie."

"Ellie," he repeated. "Not L.E."

She offered a weak little smile. "I did wonder why you were enunciating it so clearly."

Ty stared at her, and Ellie tried not to liquefy under that dark-chocolate gaze. At last, one corner of his mouth tilted up in a funny half smile.

"So, I guess I'll hold off on my spiel about double wood," he said. "That's when you leave two pins standing after the first ball, in case you're wondering."

Ellie gave an unladylike snort-laugh and buried her face in her hands. "I can't believe this conversation just happened."

"I kinda wish I'd gotten it on video," Ty said. "Again, I'm

very sorry."

Ellie looked up and shook her head. "Nothing to apologize for. I'm sure we'll both laugh about this very soon." She grinned. "Like now, maybe."

Ty grinned back, and a knot released in Ellie's chest.

"Well, then," he said at last. "Want to start again?"

# Chapter Two

"So, then Mrs. Colt said I'm not allowed to bring anything to show-and-tell unless I show it to her first."

Six-year-old Henry frowned down at his last bite of mashed potatoes, and a sharp pang zapped the center of Ellie's chest.

"It's okay, sweetie," she assured him. "We all make mistakes sometimes. Maybe you could ask me the next time you want to show someone the *How Babies Are Made* book?"

Across the table, Ellie's brother Jason was trying unsuccessfully to stifle a laugh. "I do know the mailman enjoyed it," he offered.

"So did all the ladies in my prenatal yoga class," Miriam added. "They found the pictures especially enlightening."

Ellie sighed and wondered if it was too early in the evening to pour herself a second glass of wine. "Maybe we all need to start frisking him before he leaves the house. All this time I've been assuming the only thing in his backpack was juice and goldfish crackers."

"Juice, goldfish crackers, and a stash of porn," Jason said.

"It's what's in every man's briefcase."

Henry looked up at his uncle. "What's a porn?"

"Jason!" Ellie snapped. "I've told you not to make jokes like that in front of him."

Ellie's brother had the good sense to look ashamed, though he was probably laughing inside. "Sorry, little man," Jason said. "Please erase that from your brain."

Henry pantomimed rubbing an eraser over his forehead, and Ellie laughed. No matter how crazy her life as a single mom might be, her kid always managed to make her smile.

"Mommy, may I be excused?"

"Yes, you may," Ellie said. "Remember what I showed you about rinsing off your plate before putting it in the dishwasher?"

"Uh-huh. I was just gonna lick it off, though."

"That's my boy," Jason said as Henry stood up and headed to the kitchen.

As soon as her son was out of earshot, Ellie rolled her eyes at her brother across the table. "You shouldn't encourage him."

"The kid's a cancer survivor," Jason pointed out. "He deserves to read sex books and lick plates every now and then."

Ellie's breath caught in her throat, and a wave of nausea rocked her back in the chair. Even now, a full year after Henry had been declared cancer-free, the memory of what he'd been through made her gut clench. She took a sip of water and fought to hold it together. Henry was out of the dark. There was no need to panic. Her baby was alive and happy and thriving.

"Speaking of sex books," Miriam began, and Ellie silently thanked her sister-in-law for her talent at draining the tension from any conversation. "I want to hear your Ty story again. Come on, don't leave out any details this time."

Jason stood up and pushed his chair in. "This is where I make my exit. My nephew and I are going to go do man stuff like scratching ourselves and belching and watching Batman."

"Have fun with that." Ellie watched her brother go, grateful he was such a terrific father figure to her son, even if he was sort of a butthead sometimes.

Henry's dad walked out when the boy was just a baby, and Jason had been a godsend during the leukemia battle. In a way, Ellie was relieved Chuck had chosen to leave. The fewer deadbeat jerks in Henry's life, the better.

"Come on, buddy," Jason called in the other room. "Let's go watch another episode."

A flurry of footsteps ensued, followed by the slamming of a bedroom door. Confident the boys were out of earshot, Ellie turned back to her sister-in-law, who was regarding her expectantly.

"I'm *not* repeating that story," Ellie said. "God, I don't want to relive it."

"Ty asked me again to apologize on his behalf," Miriam said. "He was super mortified."

A delighted shudder ran through her at the sound of Ty's name, but Ellie managed to avoid doing anything dumb, like drooling on the table.

"It's fine, just like I told him," Ellie insisted. "I sell sex toys for a living. I'm obviously not offended by dirty talk, especially the unintentional kind."

"That's what I explained to him." Miriam rested a hand on her pregnant belly and took a sip of her grape juice, which Ellie had poured into a wineglass so her sister-in-law could still feel fancy. "Anyway," Miriam continued, "did Ty give you some good info?"

"He gave me something, all right." Ellie's cheeks warmed, and she wanted to smack herself. Seriously, how out of practice was she? "Sorry, I shouldn't ogle your colleagues."

Miriam laughed. "I promise not to tell. So, you thought he was hot?"

Ellie's face got warmer, and she took a sip of water to cover. "I suppose he's attractive if you're into the whole tall, dark, and ridiculously handsome thing."

Miriam nodded. "He's a war vet, too."

A war vet? That was interesting. Ellie could picture it, actually. There was something a little haunted in those dark eyes. Something noble, too, or maybe she was projecting. Aside from her brother, there hadn't been that many noble men in her life.

"He definitely seemed to know his stuff," Ellie said. "Marketing stuff, I mean. And bowling balls." She smiled at the memory, wondering how he might have approached the conversation differently if he'd known what she really sold.

"He's ridiculously smart," Miriam agreed. "And a hard worker."

Ellie did her best not to release the dreamy sigh welling in her chest. "Smart, hot, good work ethic, war hero—God, women must chase him down the street to throw their panties at him."

Miriam looked thoughtful. "Actually, I don't think he dates much." She shrugged. "He never talks about it, anyway."

"Huh." Ellie was dying to ask more about him but didn't want to be too obvious. She settled for changing the subject. "Did I tell you I had a voicemail from Chuck?"

Miriam frowned. "What did the sperm donor want?"

Ellie smiled, appreciating that Miriam never called Henry's father his "dad." Chuck sure as hell hadn't earned the title.

"He wants to make changes to his child support payments," Ellie continued. "The state garners part of his wages every month. There's this complicated formula based on his income and how much time Henry spends with each parent."

"Which is zero time in his case, right?"

"Right," Ellie said. "Anyway, I haven't called him back. I'd rather just let the state handle him. I don't want to give him the chance to try and sweet talk me into taking less for Henry."

"Good girl," Miriam said. "Way to stick to your guns."

"Thanks. I'm trying. I just wish he weren't such a bastard. Henry's such a great kid, and Chuck wants nothing to do with him."

"His loss. Truly." Miriam winced, and Ellie guessed the baby had probably just socked her sister-in-law right in the bladder. Ellie remembered that feeling. She'd loved being pregnant with Henry, even with the swollen ankles and weird cravings for things like arugula and cheesy eggs.

"So," Miriam said when her grimace had faded. "Henry's healthy. Your business is booming. You're looking great."

"Thanks." Ellie smiled. "I've been biking more now that Henry's in school. It's so nice to get back to something I've always loved."

"I swear, you and Jason must have been born wearing cycling jerseys and ski boots with a tennis racquet clutched in each hand."

"Please." Ellie gave a mock shudder. "I'm way too uncoordinated for tennis. But I do love getting out on my bike again."

"Smart mama. All the parenting books I'm reading talk about the importance of hobbies and self-care."

"It does make a difference." A flicker of pride warmed Ellie's core as she thought about how hard she'd worked to reach this point. To survive divorce and Henry's cancer and to carve out a happy, healthy place for the two of them.

"So life's going great for you," Miriam said.

"Uh-huh," Ellie said, not sure where this was headed.

"Ever think about dating again?"

Ellie shrugged and tried to keep her expression casual. "Sometimes. Starting a relationship is tough when you have a kid."

"Who said anything about a relationship? I'm talking about a hookup."

"You mean like a fling?" Ellie noticed her voice sounded more intrigued than scandalized.

"Sure! Just dipping your toe in the water again."

She smiled and glanced down at her hands. "It's not my toe that's out of practice."

Miriam laughed and sipped her grape juice. "When's the last time you tried the casual thing?"

"Um, that would be never."

"Ever?"

"Nope." Ellie shook her head and tried not to be embarrassed. "Not even before I met Chuck."

"Seriously?" Miriam gaped at her. "Girl, we've gotta get you laid!"

Ellie rolled her eyes, even though the idea shot tiny little sparks of excitement through her veins. "Why do you think I sell vibrators for a living?"

"Good point." Miriam grinned. "But the toys you use with a partner are a lot more fun."

"I'll have to take your word for it."

Miriam studied her, her expression calculating. "You're not interested in a relationship?"

"Not really." Ellie shook her head and tried not to let her smile falter. Not to let her mind wander too far down the path that started with her ex-husband leaving and ended with Ellie swearing she'd never go through that kind of heartache again.

She shrugged and met her sister-in-law's gaze. "I don't think I'm ready for a boyfriend. Even that word sounds so stupid. Like I'm in fourth grade expecting someone to pull my pigtails or hand me a note with little checkboxes."

Miriam laughed. "Don't knock hair-pulling as a sign of affection."

"Please don't feel like you need to elaborate," Ellie said. "That's my brother you're getting kinky with."

"Who said anything about kink? He spent the whole first trimester holding my hair back while I hurled."

"Oh." Not for the first time, Ellie wondered if she spent entirely too much time immersed in the language of sexual aids. "Well, anyway, I'm not after a relationship. Not after what I went through with Chuck."

"But you'd be game for a fling?"

Ellie glanced down the hall. Even though she heard Jason and Henry singing the Batman theme song at full volume, she still lowered her voice to answer the question. "Maybe a fling."

Miriam grinned. "So you want me to keep an eye out for a suitable candidate?"

Ellie eyed her sister-in-law with a growing sense of wariess. And a tiny bit of giddiness. But mostly wariness. "Why do I sense you've already got someone in mind?"

Miriam's grin turned to a smirk, and Ellie didn't have to ask what she was thinking. She had a hunch.

And she had a hunch she'd be seeing him on Tuesday evening.

• • •

"Hey, Ellie." Ty held the door open as the divine Ms. Sanders wheeled through the side door, pushing a cart teeming with pink plastic crates. All of them had lids, and Ty found himself wondering what was inside.

And what was under her dress. It was white with little green flowers, and the hem fluttered up as a breeze followed her into the narrow corridor.

"Thanks so much." She brushed a handful of long, blond hair off her forehead and flashed Ty a smile that made his heart give a pleasant little sigh. "If you can leave the door propped open for just a couple minutes, I'll get everything inside in just a few trips."

"How about I give you a hand."

He didn't phrase it as a question and didn't give her a chance to argue as he hustled out to her station wagon and grabbed four more of the pink crates. They weren't terribly heavy, and he thought maybe he heard something buzzing in one of them.

"You're the best." Ellie took a turn at holding the door then fell into step beside him as he headed down the hall. "This kind of thing is so much easier with two people."

"That's what Miriam told me. She said you might need a hand."

Was it his imagination, or did her cheeks pinken just a little when he said that?

"Only if you're willing," she said. "You definitely don't have to stick around or anything."

He laughed and led her around a corner and down the hall toward the conference room. "I wasn't planning to hang out and shop for fuzzy handcuffs, but I can at least help you get set up."

"I appreciate it. Would you mind if I stuck a few signs in the hallway out there to point the way to the room?"

"Be my guest." Ty flipped on the lights, bathing the bright red conference table in a warm amber glow. The table had been Miriam's idea, and it had seemed a little bold to Ty at the start. Now, watching Ellie unpack boxes of lotion and feather ticklers, the bold hue seemed fitting.

Ty glanced away, not sure he wanted to see what else was in those boxes. He was more than a little turned on in the presence of a sexy single mom, which was a bad idea on so many levels.

"What else can I do to help?" he asked.

"Would you mind giving me a hand with that smaller table over there? I'd like to move it to the front of the room and lay out a few of the products."

"No problem."

They worked together in companionable silence, shuffling tables and moving boxes and hauling in more stuff. She was surprisingly strong, waving off his offer to help heft a large, oblong box. She hummed while she worked, a soft, lilting melody that made Ty long for lullabies he'd never heard as a kid. He caught a whiff of oranges and wondered if it was her shampoo or her breakfast. Either way, something about it soothed him.

As Ellie began unpacking one of the pink crates, Ty thought maybe he should avert his gaze.

"Holy cow." He stared as his urge to be discreet was shoved aside by his urge to know what the hell some of this stuff was. "I had no idea there was this much variety in fake penises."

"Impressive, huh?" Ellie held up a green plastic object that could be an oversize zucchini. Ty took a step back.

"That's one word for it." He cleared his throat. "Looks like you're just about set up here, so I'll go ahead and get out of your—"

"Oh, goody! A *man*!"

Ty turned as four women filed into the room. They wore huge smiles and colorful leggings with sweaters. Three of them held bottles of wine, and the fourth gripped an impressive column of clear plastic glasses.

A petite redhead in jeans at the back of the pack caught Ty's gaze on the wine and gave him a reassuring smile. "Don't worry," she said as she hoisted her bottle of Chardonnay. "We took an Uber here, so no one's driving."

A stunning African-American woman strode through the door looking like Halle Berry with a plate of brownies. "Stacy and Charlotte and Joanne are right behind us in a taxi," she announced, surveying the room. As her gaze landed on Ty, she broke into a Cheshire cat smile. "Oooh, what do we have here?" She eyed Ty up and down before turning to Ellie. "I didn't know there'd be men at this party."

"Oh, don't worry," Ellie said. "Ty was just helping me get set up, but he's on his way out."

"Worry?" A blonde woman in the corner laughed as she poured herself a generous glass of red wine. "Honey, you think anyone's worried about having a hot guy in the room?"

A pretty brunette began setting out paper plates printed with a man's naked torso. "Pretty sure every single one of us has been to sex toy parties before," she said. "But I'm betting nobody's done one with a sexy male spokesmodel."

"Hear, hear!" shouted a petite Asian woman who would probably need a step stool to look Ty in the eye. "Might be fun to get a guy's perspective for a change."

Ellie glanced at Ty with a nervous expression. He shrugged, not sure whether he should be putting up a fight or offering to stick around. If it meant he got to be with Ellie for the evening, the latter might not be so bad.

"Is he going to take off his shirt?"

Ty glanced away from Ellie to see a grandmotherly-looking woman staring at him with undisguised eagerness. "Because I was at a bachelorette party a few weeks ago, and a man showed up pretending to be a pizza delivery guy and then he took his clothes off."

"That's not the plan," Ellie assured her. "We don't usually involve men at all in Madame Butterfly parties."

Ty turned his attention back to Ellie, admiring the way she took charge of the room. Somehow she managed to be soft and sweet and authoritative all at once. Maybe it was a mom thing.

"Honey, we know," the grandma said, sidling close to Ellie and lowering her voice to a conspiratorial whisper Ty heard anyway. "But trust me on this one—we're all here because we're looking for something a little—*different*."

Grandma gave a suggestive eyebrow waggle and patted Ty fondly on the butt. He stifled the urge to flex as Ellie watched with an expression that was somewhere between horror and amusement.

Halle Berry finished dishing up brownies and stepped over to survey Ty again. Then she turned to the assembly of ladies. "Raise your hands, girls, if you've been to a sex toy party before."

Ty glanced around the room, surprised to see about two-dozen women had congregated while he'd been busy staring at Ellie. Every single one of them had a hand in the air. Clearly, Ellie Sanders had tapped into a hot market.

*Smart woman,* he thought, his admiration growing.

"So we've all been to these parties before," Grandma said, sounding triumphant. "But how many of you have ever had a little man-candy there?"

No one's hand went up, but the redhead looked at Ty and nodded. "I sure wouldn't mind trying something new."

"Then it's settled," announced a brunette with a teeming glass of white wine. "The man stays."

Ellie bit her lip and stepped toward Ty. She touched his arm and angled up to whisper in his ear, and Ty found himself stooping down to get closer.

"I'm so sorry," she whispered. "I'm sure they're just teasing. You don't have to stick around. This wasn't supposed to happen."

She was still biting her lip, which made him wonder how those lips would feel pressed up against his.

*What is wrong with you? Stop thinking about kissing her.*

Even nervous, she was so beautiful. He wanted to pull her into his arms and kiss her senseless. He also had an unsettling urge to help her out with whatever she might need. What did she need?

"This is your first party here," he whispered. "Would having me around be a help or a hindrance?"

Ellie glanced back at the crowd, uncertainty in her eyes. "A help." Her gaze slid back to his then down, and her throat moved as she swallowed. "Probably a big one."

Ty grinned. "I'll admit I kinda hate doing public presentations," he said. "But something tells me I wouldn't be expected to do much talking."

"You're probably right." She gave a shaky smile. "I don't want to inconvenience you."

Ty stepped closer, loving the way she shivered when he did. "What do *you* want, Ellie?" he whispered.

She looked startled then flushed deep crimson. It occurred to Ty he might need to clarify.

"Would you like me to stick around, or make myself scarce?" he added.

She seemed to hesitate. She glanced back at the two-dozen women who were staring at Ty like he'd just poured melted chocolate over his abs and offered them marshmallows for dipping.

"They *do* seem to want it," she murmured.

"Do you?"

He wasn't even sure what he was asking anymore, but he saw the answer in her eyes. Her cheeks were flushed and so close to his that her hair tickled his chin as she nodded once.

"Okay, then," he murmured. "I'll stay."

Someone tugged the hem of his T-shirt, and Ty turned to see the grandmotherly woman peering up at him.

"Young man." She held up an iPhone in a sparkly turquoise case. "May I take a picture with you?"

"A picture?"

"Yes, it's for my granddaughter. I've been telling her how I plan to get a hot young stud for a boyfriend. She'd simply *die* if I sent her a photo of the two of us together."

Ty laughed, even though part of him ached with nostalgia. He'd had a spirited grandmother once upon a time. She'd taught him to skip rocks and spit off bridges and curse like a thesaurus-wielding sailor. He'd wanted to live with her forever instead of just when his dad was behind bars. But she'd passed away, leaving Ty to spend the next decade bouncing between foster homes.

Shoving aside the unexpected sting of memory, Ty refocused on the cheerful octogenarian who clutched his T-shirt. "I'd be happy to help you out, Mrs...."

"Sievers," she said. "Mimi Sievers." She glanced down at the fabric in her hand, then back up at him with a hopeful expression. "Maybe you'd be willing to take your shirt off?"

"Oh, Mrs. Sievers." Ellie stepped forward and shook her head. "We don't want to take advantage of Ty."

Ty smiled, appreciating Ellie's deft handling of the situation. Corralling a bunch of tipsy party-goers wasn't easy. "It's okay," he said, turning back to his new geriatric best friend. "I don't mind, if it'll earn you some points with the granddaughter."

He grabbed the hem of his T-shirt, hesitating for an instant. He wasn't the sort of musclehead who lived to flex his pecs in public, but if it would help Ellie's sales, he was game. Hell, he'd cover his body with raspberry jam and lie on an anthill if she asked him to.

What was it about those blue eyes that made him stupid?

Ty yanked the shirt over his head in one quick movement.

"Oooh, very nice," Grandma squealed.

"That's what I'm talkin' about!" someone else shouted.

"My lord, that man is ripped."

Ty laughed, a little embarrassed. But his new surrogate grandma beamed at him like he'd handed her a chocolate cake, and the tension eased from his shoulders. He liked being of service to Mrs. Sievers. And to Ellie, who was fluttering around, handing out catalogs and stealing glances back at him.

He directed his attention back to Mrs. Sievers as she cozied up beside him, wriggling under his arm.

"Perfect," called the petite redhead as she fired off a few shots with the older woman's phone.

"Thank you, young man." Mrs. Sievers patted his butt again and sauntered off, thoroughly pleased with herself.

"My pleasure," Ty said, and wondered where his T-shirt had gone.

The brunette with the white wine stepped close to peer at the tattoo inked on his left pectoral muscle. "Is that Johnny Cash?"

*Fuck.* Another wave of memory hit Ty, this one less pleasant than the first. He remembered his dad swaying drunkenly on the sofa, belting out the wrong words to "I Walk the Line."

"It is," Ty confirmed, hoping the woman wouldn't press for more. He glanced around for his T-shirt again, finally spotting it halfway across the room. How had that happened?

Ellie watched him with heat in her eyes, and it was enough to melt the chill of memory from his veins.

"The tattoo—it's that famous photo," someone else said. "The one where Johnny is flipping off the cameraman at the concert because—"

"Okay, everyone!" Ellie called, clapping her hands at the front of the room. "Should we get started?"

He shot her a look of gratitude, admiring her crowd-handling skills. She was poised and confident and so damn beautiful it took his breath away.

She met his gaze and gave a nervous smile. "You are—

um, wow." She licked her lips. "You sure this is okay?"

"Being ogled by two-dozen horny women?" Ty lifted one eyebrow. "Yeah, I think I can handle it."

Her cheeks went a little pinker, but she nodded. "Okay, but signal me if you get uncomfortable for any reason. If you want to stop."

"What, like the Bat-Signal?"

Ellie gave him a funny look. "That's my son's favorite superhero," she said. "Batman."

Ty kept his expression neutral but said a quiet prayer of thanks for the reminder. Ellie was a mom, which made her strictly off-limits for dating.

But harmless flirtation? Maybe that was okay.

"I don't actually know how to do a Bat-Signal," he said. "But if I run screaming from the room, that's the cue I've had enough."

"Just the same, I don't want you to get uncomfortable," she said. "Especially once we start talking about toys and stuff."

"I'm fine, El. Your concern is sweet, though."

He couldn't think of a time when someone had cared about what happened to him, and being on the receiving end of it from Ellie Sanders warmed him from the inside.

"Humor me," she said. "If you get uncomfortable, just say 'I'm out.' That'll let me know I need to wrap things up and let you go. Deal?"

"Deal." Ty hesitated then reached out to take her hand in his.

"What are you doing?" she whispered.

"We're shaking hands on it."

"Oh. Right, yes, of course. Sorry, I'm a little out of practice at this."

He smiled. "You and me both."

# Chapter Three

This was insanity.

A hot, shirtless man standing next to her? Hell, his abs alone were crazynuts. He looked like something out of an underwear ad.

And the fact that he'd stripped to help her out just added to the appeal.

"Okay, ladies," Ellie said. "We're going to start off with a few items from our Tame Me bondage line. This is a great vanilla starter kit for those testing it out or those who want to experiment just a little."

"What's that?" called a pretty redhead named Jane. She was the one who'd contacted Ellie in the first place about hosting the party. Most of these women were part of the same book club, though many had brought friends.

Ellie glanced down at the object Jane was pointing at. "This is bondage tape," she explained. "It has a lot of different uses for couples looking to experiment with a little light BDSM play."

"Like what?" someone else called.

Ellie cleared her throat and ordered herself not to get embarrassed. She'd had plenty of conversations like this and was no stranger to frank discussions about sexual aids.

But she'd never had a man in the audience before. A bare-chested, insanely attractive m—

"You can use it to restrain your partner by binding his or her wrists together," Ellie said, avoiding Ty's eyes. "Or you can bind him or her to a piece of furniture."

"What about ankles?" someone called. "Would it work on ankles?"

"Absolutely," Ellie said. "Ankle-to-wrist, ankle-to-ankle—whatever feels good."

"Getting that tape stuck on arm hair wouldn't make *me* feel good," someone said, prompting a round of giggles from the audience.

"Yeah, my husband would never go for that," someone else added. "He has super hairy legs."

"That's the beauty of bondage tape," Ellie said. "It's non-adhesive. It's more of an electrostatic cling tape. You can even use it to cover someone's eyes like a blindfold."

The women looked dubious, so Ellie tore off a piece to demonstrate. "Here, I'll show you how it works." She struggled to bind her wrists together but quickly realized that wasn't going to work.

"Want help?" Ty's voice was deep and rich, like liquid chocolate. He stepped closer, so close her arms tingled from the heat of his body. He held out his hands, palms pressed together, wrists angled toward her. His eyes met hers and Ellie shivered.

"By all means," he murmured. "Use me."

*Oh, sweet baby Jesus.*

Ellie flashed back to her conversation with Miriam about flings. He didn't know, did he?

No. Miriam wouldn't do that.

Ty was just being helpful. That seemed to be his nature. Whipping his shirt off for a crowd of horny women didn't seem like something in his wheelhouse, but he'd done it to make an old woman's day. His willingness to be of service made Ellie warm with gratitude.

Okay, so that wasn't the only thing making her warm.

She took a deep breath and reached for Ty's wrists. "Thanks," she said.

Her voice came out like a squeak, and she cleared her throat as she wound the bright purple tape around those massive wrists, overlapping it and pressing firmly to secure it. Ty's arms were muscular and covered in dark hair that felt softer than she expected it to. There was a light dusting of hair on his chest, too, and Ellie wondered if it would feel springy pressed against bare breasts. *Her* bare breasts.

"There. That should be nice and snug." She stepped back, needing to put some distance between them before she climbed his body like a jungle gym.

"How do you get it off?" someone asked.

"Yes," Ty murmured, giving her a knowing look. "How *do* you get it off?"

Ellie licked her lips. "You can unwind it, of course," she said. "It's reusable. But we also sell bondage shears like these ones." She picked up the pair on the table, surprised to see her hands were shaking. "Some couples enjoy the thrill of cutting each other out of restraints. These are like the ones medical professionals use to cut bandages, so they're very safe."

"Oooh, can I try?" Mrs. Sievers hustled up, and Ellie found herself smiling. This was her ideal kind of party, when women of all ages were refreshingly open with their sexuality.

She handed the shears to the older woman, who giggled and leaned in close to cut Ty free. "Ooh, you're a big fellow, aren't you?"

Ty grinned and glanced at Ellie. "So, I've been told."

Ellie's mouth went dry. "Right." She cleared her throat. "So, uh—let's move on and talk about our lingerie line. Did everyone have a chance to look through the catalog?"

"I have a question." A shy-looking brunette in the corner had raised her hand, and Ellie nodded.

"Yes?"

"This mesh bodysuit—is this crotchless?"

"Yes," Ellie confirmed. "All the body stockings on page twelve are open between the legs."

A woman with apple-round cheeks and pretty blond curls gave a small sigh. "It says it comes in XXL, but I don't know—would my husband really want to see me in something like *that*? Or would I just look like a trussed-up sausage?"

Several women beside her tittered and patted her arm, but the woman looked up from the catalog and pointed at Ty. "No, I'm serious," she said. "I know men are visual creatures, so I'm curious if this would be a turn-on or a turn-off. You can be honest with me, sweetie—bad idea?"

Ty folded his arms over his chest and met the woman's gaze with a softness in his eyes. A softness that made Ellie's belly quiver before he even said a word.

"You're absolutely right that men are visual creatures," he said. "And we can see when you're rockin' the self-confidence. Put on that body stocking or whatever the hell you want, and tell yourself you're a sex goddess. I guarantee he'll feel the same way."

The woman beamed at him, and Ellie wanted to kiss Ty. His words were one thing, but the sincerity in his voice was enough to make every woman in the room fall head over heels for him.

*Not me. I'm not falling for anyone. No, sir.*

Ellie cleared her throat and scanned the room. Several women ticked boxes on their order forms and pointed at items on the catalog pages.

"What about toys?" one woman asked. "I've got a whole drawer full of 'em, and now that I've started dating again, I'm wondering if a guy would be freaked out if I show him."

"Maybe don't bust them out on the first date," Ty said. "But once you're well-acquainted, any man who gets freaked out by sex toys isn't much of a man."

Murmurs of approval rippled through the room, and Ellie telegraphed her gratitude to Ty. Would he take it the wrong way if she offered to buy him a beer later?

She reached into her toolbox and pulled out one of Madame Butterfly's best-selling vibrators. "This is called the Happy Jammer," she said. "It's very popular with couples because of the vibrating nodules here and here and right here—" She held it up, conscious of Ty's eyes on her as she pointed out all the parts. "It's designed to stimulate both partners," she added.

Kellyanne, a stunning African-American woman Ellie knew through her cycling club, put her hands on her hips and stared down Ty. "How about now, big guy? Threatened by something *that* size?"

Ty smiled and shook his head. "Not even close."

The woman smiled. "I think I like you."

Ty smiled back. "I'm a likable guy."

Ellie's heart bubbled in her chest.

*No kidding, buddy.*

• • •

"Thanks again for all your help." Ellie glanced at Ty and tried to decide if she was relieved or disappointed he'd put his shirt back on. At least now she faced less risk of drooling on the carpet.

"No problem," he said. "Which box should I stuff this in?"

"Uh—right here." Ellie pried open the flaps on a pink

plastic crate and as Ty deposited the Buzzy Butterfly clitoral stimulator inside. "Thanks."

Thirty minutes had passed since the last guest departed, but Ty was still here. He could be home watching TV by now, but it was a relief to have his help. At this rate she might make it home in time to tuck Henry in for the night.

"You don't have to clean up," she said. "I've got this, I swear."

"I'm atoning for my sins," he said. "For all the douchey-sounding things I said the first time we met."

"For the last time, it wasn't douchey." Ellie folded a black lace teddy and tucked it into one of her crates. "You thought you were talking about bowling balls, and I thought you were giving me tips on being a new business owner. It was an honest mistake."

He eyed her curiously for a moment. "I never actually gave you any tips, did I?"

"Sure you did. I know more now about bowling pins and ball-washing than I ever used to."

Ty laughed and closed the top on a pink crate before stacking it on her wheeled cart. "No, I mean actual entrepreneurial tips. Miriam asked me to give you a hand, and instead I talked dirty to you."

"It's fine, Ty. Although now that you've watched one of my sales presentations, I'd be interested in any feedback you have."

"I thought you did great."

He was probably being nice, but her confidence had grown the more she talked. Still, there was room for improvement.

"Seriously, I'd love your two cents on how tonight went," she said. "Public presentations are more your thing than mine."

"Video is my thing," he said. "I leave the public presentation stuff to the other partners. But if you want my opinion on that, I think you'd be terrific on camera."

Ellie snorted. "What, you mean hawking sex toys on late-night cable commercials?"

"No, I'm talking about product demos." Ty leaned back against a bank of cabinets and folded his arms over his chest. "Classy little how-to videos embedded on your website to show potential customers what something looks like or how it operates."

She grimaced and shook her head. "The women in the PTA at my son's school would have a heart attack."

"You wouldn't be broadcasting it on the five-o'clock news," he pointed out. "You could even put them in a password-protected section of your website so only trusted customers would be able to view them. And you'd keep things very tasteful."

Ellie considered it. She liked that he'd said "tasteful," which meant he wasn't suggesting she do anything too sultry or suggestive. Just the same sort of things she talked about in her presentations.

But the idea of being on camera made her queasy. She thought about bright lights and microphones and her annoying habit of tripping over her tongue when she got nervous.

Then she thought about working with Ty. Like magic, some of the queasiness evaporated.

"Is it expensive?" she asked. "Video, I mean."

"It can be," he said. "But there's a friends and family discount you'd get through Miriam."

"Really?" Ellie wondered if that was true or if he was just being nice. "That might help."

"Actually, I was wondering if you'd be open to trade."

Ellie blinked. She imagined herself exchanging sexual favors for professional editing work.

*Wait. What?* She swallowed hard. "What do you mean by trade?"

"You have a terrific voice," he said. "I was noticing that during your presentation. Great enunciation, just the right pacing. Maybe you'd be up for doing a little voiceover work."

"Voiceover work?" Her voice cracked, and she wanted to smack herself in the forehead for repeating his words like some sort of deranged parrot.

Ty, bless his heart, didn't seem fazed. "There's a whole series of commercials I'm producing over the next few weeks," he said. "I've been looking for just the right female voice to use, and I think you might be a good fit."

Ellie nodded, embarrassed by her disappointment that he wasn't propositioning her. "That sounds interesting. Is it for the bowling ball company?"

He laughed and shook his head. "Nah, it's a company that makes kombucha. Mama Jama's. I think your sound is perfect for them."

She smiled, pleased he'd noticed such an odd little detail about her. It seemed sweeter than if he'd noticed her legs or cleavage or ass.

Not that she'd mind that.

Ellie cleared her throat. "I'd be willing to give it a shot. The voiceover stuff, I mean. And maybe the video stuff."

"Great." Ty grinned and uncrossed his arms. "In that case, I look forward to working with you."

Ellie nodded, looking forward to it a whole lot more than she wanted to admit. "It's a date."

# Chapter Four

Ty fiddled with the damn boom mike again, wishing he'd had the foresight to order a new one before his first video shoot with Ellie Sanders.

All right, if he were being honest, his frustration had nothing to do with the gadget. He could just use a lavalier mike and be done with it.

No, Ty was on edge because Ellie Sanders left him reeling like a teenager with a crush. It was stupid. He'd worked with plenty of beautiful women in his career, but none made him feel like someone poured liquid fudge over his heart and handed him a spoon.

That made no sense at all. See? He was losing it, and not just because Ellie Sanders was beautiful. She was also smart and funny and sweet and *totally* off-limits. A *mother*, for crying out loud. No way would he go marching into a situation with such a risk of someone getting attached and hurt and—

Footsteps jarred Ty's attention to the front of his office, and his pulse stuttered at the sight of Ellie in his doorway.

"Hi there." She hesitated at the threshold of the studio

then shot a nervous glance at the camera. Feeling like a dick, Ty reminded himself not to ogle her. The way she stared at the equipment suggested a serious case of camera shyness.

"Don't worry," he said. "It's not on yet. We won't start rolling until you've had a chance to settle in and get comfortable."

"Unlikely to happen," Ellie said, but she stepped into the studio anyway. She smoothed her hands down the skirt of a knee-length, pale blue dress with triangle-shaped cutouts on the sides, and Ty wondered what good thing he'd done in a past life to deserve this kind of view.

"That's a great dress," he said, and ordered himself not to imagine what it might look like puddled on the floor at her feet.

"It's not too much? Miriam told me to dress a little sexy, but I'm so out of practice at sexy that I wasn't sure whether to put on clean yoga pants or wrap my body in Saran Wrap."

"You pretty much nailed it," Ty said, adding the Saran Wrap image to his mental spank bank. God, there were a lot of images of Ellie Sanders in there. "There is one small problem, though."

"What's that?"

Ty lifted the mike. "Normally I'd set up a shotgun mike on a boom to record the sound for the test shoot. But I'm having trouble with the clips."

"So we aren't going to film, then?"

The hope on her face almost made him laugh, but laughter wouldn't do much to help her nerves.

"We're still shooting, but not until you're ready," he said. "My plan was to hook you up to a lavalier mike."

"What's a lavalier mike?"

"It has a little microphone that clips to a collar or the front of a dress. There's a wire that feeds through your clothes and leads to a transmitter hooked to your belt or waistband."

"Oh." Ellie looked down at the dress, which clearly had no belt or waistband. "I'm sorry."

"No, it's fine! Don't worry about it. We'll just have to get creative."

Ty picked up the mike pack and studied the back of Ellie's dress. "Maybe if you try pinching a little fabric in back?"

"Sure." She contorted her arms behind her and made a valiant grab for the small of her back. The material slipped from her fingers. Ellie tried again, an impressive display of dexterity. "Got it!"

Okay, so it was a little off-center. Still, Ty wasn't going to start putting his hands all over her. "All right, I'm just going to clip this right here."

He held the wires and mike in one hand and opened the jaws of the clip on the mike pack. He clamped them onto the fabric—something silky and soft. Almost as soft as Ellie's hand, which he grazed as he let go of the clamp.

"There," he said. "That should—*gah! Goddamn egg-whacking piss-wizard!*"

He reached out and caught the transmitter, halting its plummet to the floor. "Sorry for the language."

Ellie laughed. "Sometime within the hour, I'm going to be talking to the camera about sex toys. I'm hardly worried about a few creative curse words." She gave him a curious look. "Where'd you learn to swear like that?"

A dark cloud seeped into his consciousness, but he fought to keep it from showing on his face. "My grandmother."

She rested a hand on one of his high-backed chairs and regarded him with interest. "She sounds like a unique woman."

His throat was tight, so Ty just nodded. Nodded and reminded himself what it felt like to say good-bye to her—to his grandmother and to all the foster parents and foster siblings who'd followed. It was one of sixteen-thousand reasons he shouldn't be thinking illicit thoughts about Ellie Sanders.

"She was." Ty cleared his throat. "I wish I'd had her around longer."

"I'm so sorry." She touched his hand, and the sincerity in her voice was like a warm balm on his heart. "Losing someone you care about is such an awful experience."

*Exactly.* That's exactly why he shouldn't be flirting with Ellie Sanders. Mentally, he thanked her for the reminder, even though his heart wanted to soak up her kindness like a sponge.

Looking away, he gripped the mike pack in one hand. "Would you mind if I took another stab at clipping this on you?"

"Please, go right ahead. Obviously, I can't reach very well."

"Okay." He took a step closer and pinched a large swatch of fabric together, careful not to let his fingers graze the bare skin showing through the cutouts on the side of the dress. The silky fabric was warm from her body, and Ty's hands were unsteady as he clamped the mike pack onto it.

"There," he said. "How does that feel?"

"Um, a little tight."

Ellie frowned down at the front of her dress. The outline of her breasts was a whole lot clearer now than it had been before, something Ty didn't mind in the least.

But he recognized that Ellie was uncomfortable.

"Sorry," she said, plucking at the front of her dress. "I'm a little self-conscious."

"Right. Sorry about that." Crap, he definitely didn't want her any more uncomfortable than she already was. He released the clip on the mike pack and tried again with a smaller swatch of fabric. "There. How does that feel?"

"Better. Thank you."

"No problem. Okay, now we need to thread this wire up through the dress and—"

"You mean under my clothes?"

"Yes. Don't worry; I'll turn around to give you some privacy. You can try threading it up the side, though I guess that might be a problem with the wire showing through." He gestured to the cutouts, and Ellie smoothed her hands self-consciously over them.

"Sorry. I really should have planned better. I can run home and change if you—"

"No! We can make this work." He cleared his throat. "Okay, what if you, uh—threaded the wire from the back up through the front—"

"You mean between my legs?"

"Right. Yes, that would do it."

God, it was hot in the studio. Ty thought about opening a window, but that would seriously fuck with the sound. He handed Ellie the wire and the mike and took a few steps back. "I'll just turn around, okay? You got it?"

"I think so." She seemed uncertain, and Ty wondered if there was any way of salvaging this, of putting her at ease.

He turned his back, hoping a little privacy might help her. "Shout when you pull the wire through, and I'll help you hook the mike to the front."

"Thank you."

Ty took a few deep breaths and thought about football, grilling techniques for cheeseburgers, and whether he needed to do laundry. Anything but the image of Ellie with her hand sliding up her thighs and under her dress and—

"Shoot!"

Her tame expletive was tinged with frustration, and there was a clatter behind him as something hit the floor.

"You okay?" he asked in a voice that didn't quite sound like his own.

"I dropped the thingy," she said. "The box that you'd hooked to the back of my dress? I'm sorry. It just came off."

"No problem. Is it safe to turn around?"

"Yes. Sorry."

"No worries." Ty turned back around, relieved to see her dress in place and the mike pack all in one piece. "My fault," he assured her. "I knew that fabric was probably too slippery. Let's try something else."

He stepped toward her again, inspecting the dress—not her body, dammit—as closely as he dared. Those cutouts at the waistline were sexy as hell, but not sturdy enough to hold the weight of the mike pack. "Okay, what if you hooked it to your, uh…your…"

He froze, not wanting to make this more awkward than it already was.

Ellie frowned, uncomprehending. "My what?"

"Your, um…"

A small smile flickered in her eyes. "Is this like charades with body parts and articles of clothing?"

There was a teasing note in her voice, and Ty reminded himself which business she was in. It wasn't like he was going to offend her.

"Your underwear," he said. "Panties."

Ellie laughed. "Yeah, one problem with that."

"What?"

"I'm wearing a super-tiny thong. More of a G-string, I guess."

*Holy mother of—*

"Okay, then." Ty cleared his throat, grateful he couldn't see the expression on his face.

But Ellie saw it, and it made her laugh again. "I wasn't trying to be sexy or anything," she said. "These cutouts dip too low on the sides, so regular panties wouldn't work. And the lace is pretty flimsy, so I don't think—"

"Okay!" Ty said again, a little too loudly this time. His brain was buzzing, and he definitely needed to turn up the air conditioning, or maybe just stop thinking about Ellie Sanders's underwear. "Let's try something else."

"What if I just held the box thingy in my hand while I talk?"

Ty shook his head. "It tends to inhibit people's ability to be expressive. To use their hands when they talk. Besides, won't you need your hands to show some of the merchandise?"

"Good point." Ellie frowned. "How about my bra?"

"Great idea! That's probably sturdier."

Ellie gave him a wry look. "I don't know about that. I'm not exactly big enough to require any heavy-duty support. But at least that should be more secure. You want the mike thingy hooked in back, right?"

"Right. That's definitely best."

"Okay, then I'm going to need your help."

Ty swallowed hard and stood rooted to the floor. "How do you mean?"

"Well, without taking my dress off, I can't quite get to my bra clasp to hook something on it. Besides, I'm not sure my arms will even bend like that."

"Of course, you're right." He needed water, either to drink or to dump over his head. Maybe both. "Okay, let me think for a second."

There was no zipper up the back, so maybe it just pulled on? "Um, does this thing have a zipper?"

"Yes, it's up the side. Want me to undo it?"

*Oh, God.*

She gave an embarrassed little smile and touched his arm, sending electric currents pulsing all the way to his groin.

"It's fine, Ty," she said. "I think modesty is sort of a moot point by now, don't you?"

Before he could say anything, she was reaching under her

right arm and tugging the zipper down. Sheer, cream-colored lace appeared where the pale blue fabric parted, and Ty caught a glimpse of smooth satin that curved over her breast. He started to glance away then realized there was no possible way to do this without looking.

"There," she said. "Is that enough, or should I go more?"

"I think that'll do it." His voice came out like a croak, and he wanted to punch himself in the face. Instead, he stepped closer and took the mike pack from her, grateful his hands seemed steady. He hesitated then reached for the opening in her dress.

"Oh, good—your hands aren't cold." She turned and grinned at him.

"Cold? It's like three million degrees in here."

"Really? I'm kind of chilly."

Ty didn't mean to let his gaze drop to the front of her dress, but oh-sweet-lord, she was definitely cold. He glanced away fast.

"Would you mind if I tugged this zipper down just another inch or so?"

"Go right ahead," she said. "Here, I can help—"

She turned to reach under her arm, and the movement pushed her breast right into the back of his hand. *Soft.* So fucking soft Ty could scarcely breathe, but he ordered himself to stay conscious as she inched the zipper down farther.

"There," she said. "Let me know if you need more."

Oh, he needed more, that was for damn sure. *God.* The fact that she was sexy as hell was bad enough. But her sweetness, her charm, her openness about sexuality—how did all those mismatched things fit so perfectly into one beautiful package?

Ty swallowed and tried to gain control of himself.

"Okay, I'm just going to reach into the back of your dress," he said. "Let me know if I pinch you or anything."

"You're doing great."

Now *she* was reassuring *him*?

Some professional he was.

Ty slid his hand around her back, his fingers grazing the narrow ridge of her shoulder blade as he skimmed over her bra strap and found the clasp in the center of her spine. Her skin was unbearably soft, and so warm. He hoped to God his fingers still worked as he fumbled the mike clip open and hooked it to the bra.

"There!" he announced a little too enthusiastically. "Okay, I'm going to leave the rest to you." He drew his hand out of her dress, taking the wire and the mike with it. He handed both to her. "You can either thread this around the side under your...um..."

"Breast?"

"Right. Or you can go over your shoulder. I think going under would be less restrictive to your movement, but it's up to you."

"I've got this," she said.

Before Ty averted his gaze, she'd pulled her dress open farther, exposing the side of her breast. It was cupped in lace and satin and quite possibly the most beautiful body part Ty had ever seen in his life.

*And that is not an exaggeration.*

Ellie caught his eye and gave an apologetic shrug. "I'd be showing more flesh in a bikini on a beach," she said. "We're both adults here."

"Right," Ty croaked. "That we are."

Ty found it impossible to look away as she snaked the wire under her bra then reached into her dress, between her breasts, and threaded the mike out through the neckline. Holding it up triumphantly, she grinned at him.

"There. That wasn't so hard."

*Oh, yes. Yes, it was.*

• • •

Truth. Ellie wanted Ty to notice the dress she'd splurged on.

But she'd never imagined he'd have his hands inside it, or that he'd end up accidentally cupping her breast.

*Bonus.*

Her lower regions warmed. It had been a while since anything like that had happened, and this was *so* not the time.

"What are all these lights for?" She glanced up at bulbs, trying to focus on something besides Ty. Spots danced in front of her eyes, and she blinked to clear her vision.

"They ensure the picture is crystal clear and we don't have any weird colors or shadows on your face," he said. "It's important to get the lighting just right for your size and shape and skin tone and what you're wearing."

"It's okay," Ellie said, and it really was. She was in no hurry for him to turn on the cameras.

*Ugh.* A queasy ick spread through her middle.

Ever since the third grade, when she forgot her lines in the school production of *Hansel and Gretel,* doing anything for an audience put her nerves on edge. That's one reason she found Madame Butterfly so fun. She sat behind a computer screen and interacted with people virtually.

But if she wanted to grow the business, this was necessary. The party the other night had been a success, but video seemed like the right next move. And it was generous of Ty to offer his help.

He was bent down adjusting a cable, which gave her a prime view. He had an amazing ass, well-muscled and perfectly curved in jeans. It was the sort of butt a woman might dig her claws into as he drove into her with—

"How does that feel?"

Ellie blinked. "What?"

"Is that too hot with all the lights on?"

"No. I'm okay."

"You look a little flushed."

"I'm good."

*Nice, Ellie. If you can't construct a sentence of more than three words, this video thing is going to go great.*

She crossed and uncrossed her legs. Her hands shook, and she wasn't quite sure what to do with them.

"We're almost ready," he said. "How about you say a few words for sound check."

"Words?" she repeated like an idiot. *Where are my words?*

Ass. Eyes. Arms. Chest.

*No. Don't say those words.*

"How about introducing yourself," he suggested.

"Okay." She bit her lip. "Hi, I'm Shelly Anders and—"

Crap, that wasn't her name.

Ty looked at her like she had three heads.

"Oh, you wanted words that made sense?" She managed a weak little smile, then licked her lips and tried again. "Hi, I'm Ellie Sanders." Her voice wobbled a little on the last syllable, and she had no clue what to say next. "Um—I like carrots, thunderstorms, and the smell of bark dust."

Dear God, she sounded like a contestant on a bad dating show. The lights blazed around her, but she was chilled to the bone.

Ty grinned, glancing away once to adjust something on the camera.

"Tell me the name of your company," he said.

"Madame Butterfly."

*Yay! I got one right.*

"And what do they sell?" he prompted. Then he gave her a small smile. "Besides bowling balls, I mean."

Ellie laughed. Well, she tried. She choked on her own spit.

Ty whacked her on the back, careful not to hit the mike thingy. "Are you okay?"

Ellie nodded and sputtered. She was the worst on-camera client in the history of all time. Ty moved his hand from her back and seemed to hesitate there for a moment. Probably thinking about suggesting a nice brochure or e-newsletter. Anything that didn't involve Ellie being in front of a camera.

He turned and grabbed a high-backed barstool identical to the one Ellie was sitting on. He dragged it over so he was sitting beside her. When he spoke, his voice was low and soothing.

"I can tell the camera is making you nervous," he said.

Ellie rolled her eyes. "You think?"

"I get it," he said. "I'm prone to stage fright, too. I hate talking in front of crowds. Or doing any kind of public presentation."

The confession put her at ease a little. Ellie took a few deep breaths, hoping to make the dizziness go away. "I'm sorry. I feel dumb."

"Don't. We just need to make you more comfortable." He smiled and scooted a little closer. Their knees almost touched. "How about we try this. I'm just going to sit right here, and we're going to chat like normal people."

"You mean normal people who don't forget their own names and choke on saliva?"

"Something like that."

Ellie spit a hunk of hair out of her mouth and glanced at the camera again. "I'm horrible at this."

"I've seen worse."

"Really?"

He paused for a moment, and Ellie figured he was rethinking his assertion. "I didn't start out in marketing," he said. "I was a mass communications specialist making videos in the Navy."

"I didn't know the Navy had videos."

"Yeah, training stuff, documentation, that sort of thing.

Anyway, I had to interview this vice-admiral once for a piece we were doing on tactical operations." His voice was low and soothing, and Ellie leaned into it. "Admiral Branson insisted on standing, even though the angle we'd set up had him sitting on a bench. And anytime one of us would open our mouths to offer any kind of feedback, he'd bark at us to stay quiet unless he told us it was okay to speak."

"Sounds like kind of a jerk." Ellie's shoulders started to relax, and she leaned back a little in her chair, eager to hear the rest of his story.

"Yeah, the military's full of guys like that." Ty smiled. "A few seconds after the camera starts rolling, I notice the guy's fly is down. Not just a little, either. Like gaping open, showing off his tighty-whiteys. I raise my hand and say, 'Pardon me, sir—' That's all I managed to get out before he barked at me to 'Shut it, son!' Told me if he heard another word out of me, he'd have me written up."

"What did you do?"

Ty shrugged. "What could I do? I tried giving him the universal, 'barn door's open' signal, but he was staring straight ahead and into the camera. When he finished up, I tried to tell him about his wardrobe malfunction. I was going to give him the chance to reshoot."

"Was he embarrassed?" Ellie crossed her legs, so engrossed in the story she'd nearly forgotten the spotlights and camera.

"He never let me get the words out," Ty said. "Just barked, 'Out of my way!' and marched out of the room."

"Jeez," Ellie said. "So did you have to scrap the footage?"

"Nah, I got creative. Put a graphic with his name and rank over his crotch and made it look like we'd planned it that way all along. The guy never knew."

"That's so sweet." Something about the story was weirdly touching. How many guys would have seized the chance to let the guy make an ass of himself after he'd been such a jerk to start with?

But not Ty. Ty had shown the guy respect, even when he hadn't shown him any.

He seemed to read her thoughts. "I believe in karma," he said. "If you take the chance to be a jerk to someone, someone's bound to do the same to you. Stop the flow of assholery and respond with kindness instead, and you'll eventually get the same in return."

"Wow," she said. "That's a great theory. I kind of wish my ex subscribed to it."

Shit. She hadn't meant to say that. Badmouthing the father of her child was never a good idea, no matter who she was talking to, but it was especially dumb in front of the guy she was assessing for fling potential.

"Sorry," she said. "I didn't mean to be one of those bitter divorced women. I take great pains to never say anything negative to Henry about his father. I've just…it's been a rough week."

Ty studied her face for a moment without saying anything. Ellie fought the urge to look away, focusing on his eyes instead. He had beautiful eyes. The first time they'd met, she'd mistaken them for coal black, but they were actually more of a mahogany, like coffee beans or tanned leather or her mother's walnut cookies.

"Want to talk about it?" Ty murmured.

She'd forgotten what they were discussing. Cookies? No, her asshole ex. Ellie shook her head, annoyed with herself for bringing it up. "Not really," she said. "Just a conflict about child support. As in, he'd prefer not to pay any."

Ty's expression clouded. Those dark eyes turned molten, and his hands clench into fists.

"Corn-sucking ass badger," he muttered. "I fucking hate guys like that."

Ellie blinked. "Um, yeah. I see that."

Ty waved a hand. "Sorry, that's sort of a sore spot for me."

"You have kids?"

"No."

His voice was flat. She needed to change the subject, but she had no idea what to say.

"I had an asshole dad of my own," he said. "I get pissed when I hear about guys abandoning their kids. It's like — Jesus. They have no idea what that does to a kid to be left like that."

Ellie looked at him, touched that he'd share such a personal detail. Something about the timbre of his voice, the darkness in his eyes, told her he didn't do that often. "I've tried to minimize the impact on Henry," she said softly. "Having his dad leave, I mean."

"Good," Ty said. "You sound like a great mother."

He watched her a moment, then leaned back a little, almost like he was trying to put some space between them.

"Anyway, sorry about the cursing," he said. "Hearing about fathers like that brings out the jerk in me." He gave a brittle laugh. "Or maybe that's the DNA. Jerk behavior is pre-ordained."

Ellie cocked her head to the side, intrigued by that line of thinking. "You mean you believe people are destined to morph into their parents?"

Ty looked at her for a long time. Ellie held her breath and wondered how they'd gone off on this tangent. They were supposed to be making sex toy videos, not discussing weighty subjects like divorce and DNA.

But he'd been trying to put her at ease, and this was helping. Strange as it seemed, sitting here chatting with Ty under the bright studio lights was almost natural. Nice, even.

"Let me ask you something," he said at last. "What's your kid's favorite lunch?"

The question startled her, and it took Ellie a second to

answer. "Peanut butter and jelly sandwiches," she said. "Only, I take the bread and flatten it with a rolling pin, and then I cover it with peanut butter and jelly and sometimes thin slices of banana, if I have it. Then I roll it up like a jelly roll and tuck it in one of those snack bags for his lunch. He loves it."

Ty smiled, and there was something wistful in his eyes. "I was right," he said. "You are a great mom. Where'd you learn to do that?"

"The mom-ing or the sandwich?"

"Both."

"My mom, I guess." Ellie shifted in her seat, her chest rattling with loss and longing at the memory of her mother. "On both counts."

"That's what I'm talking about." Ty spread his hands over his knees and stared right into her eyes. "People can't help but repeat what they learned from their own parents. Whether it's sandwiches or bedtime stories or favorite curse words. Sounds like you had a good mom."

"I did," Ellie admitted, her voice thick. "The best."

She held back, not wanting to volunteer the whole story of how her mother died when she was little, or how her big brother raised her. As much as she liked Ty, she didn't want to start down that path. Not yet, anyway.

"My mom was incredible," she said. "If I can be even half the mom she was, it'll be the proudest achievement of my life. Nothing else compares."

"There," he said. "The way your eyes lit up just then. That's perfect."

Ellie blinked. "What do you mean?"

"You're passionate about your family. About being a mom, about your own mom—it makes you light up from the inside." Ty beamed and gestured toward the camera. "That's what I want to see from you when that's rolling. I saw it the other day when you were doing your presentation, so I know you can do it."

Ellie laughed, not sure whether to feel flattered or awkward. She settled for a bit of both. "So you're saying I have the same maniacal gleam when I'm talking about my mom as I do when I'm talking about anal beads? That's disturbing."

Ty smiled and shook his head. "Tell me what you love about your company."

"It's empowering," she said, no hesitation at all. "For women in particular. So many of them have spent their whole lives thinking their sexuality is dirty or shameful. Something they're not supposed to talk about. But Madame Butterfly shows them that sex is not only normal, but fun and exciting. And they can learn things about the way their bodies work. About what gives them pleasure, and how to ask for it from their partners. I love helping women find that for themselves."

Ty raised his hands and applauded. "Perfect. Absolutely perfect."

"What?" Ellie shifted on her barstool, a flush of pride washing through her.

"What you did just then. When you relaxed and opened up and then got a little fire in your belly. That's what you need to bring to your presentations. To your on-camera presence."

Ellie glanced at the camera. She'd almost forgotten about it while they'd been talking. A cluster of butterflies stirred in her belly, but Ty's voice cut through the hum of their wings. "Uh-uh," he said. "Look at me. Not at the camera. Just forget it's there."

Ellie took a deep breath and looked back at his handsome face. Those coal-dark eyes were suddenly so familiar to her. So soothing. She'd only been sitting here with him for, what — five minutes? Ten?

But already she felt a thousand times better about this whole video thing.

Then he smiled, and a warm ball of sunshine spread from

her belly all the way to the tips of her fingers.

"You ready to try this for real now?"

She nodded. "Let's give it a shot."

• • •

Ty had just shut down the camera equipment for the day when his cell phone rang. He was planning to ignore it, figuring personal calls could wait until after business hours.

But the name on the screen sent him fumbling to answer.

"Anna, hi." Ty cleared his throat and said a silent prayer this wasn't an emergency call. That his half-sister wasn't hurt or sick or in jail or—

"I'm getting married!" she squealed.

Or that.

Ty took a deep breath, weighing his own terror at the word "married" against his sister's obvious happiness.

"That's—that's great," he managed. He sat down on the edge of his desk and summoned his most supportive-sounding voice. "Who's the lucky guy?"

"His name is Martin, and that's why I'm calling," she said. "I know I haven't seen you in ages, but I want you to meet him." She paused a little there, and Ty sensed there was more to her request. That if he just waited, she'd spit it out.

"I was hoping maybe you'd walk me down the aisle."

Her voice was almost a whisper, but it hit Ty like a ten-pound boulder to the chest. He swallowed hard, surprised to find tears clogging his throat. That made it hard to respond, which was probably why Anna scrambled to fill the silence.

"It's okay if you don't want to," she said. "I know you hate doing stuff in front of crowds, and it's not like we even grew up together."

Ty blinked hard. They'd been shuffled between separate foster homes, too young to understand what was happening.

Just when Ty would get attached, he'd get bumped someplace else, until "good-bye" was more familiar to him than "I love you." Anna's mom got out of rehab and came back to claim her, but Ty's mom was dead by then. Their father had been no use at all, bouncing between prison and—

"I'd love to," Ty said, desperate to halt the flow of dark memories. "Walk you down the aisle. I'd be honored."

He meant it, too. Marriage and kids weren't in the cards for him, but he desperately wanted Anna to be happy. If getting married would give her that, he'd do it.

"Oh, Ty. This means so much to me."

"I'm glad to help."

"I promise you won't have to do any public speaking," she said. "Just walk me down the aisle."

He laughed and shifted a little on the edge of his desk. "I'm here for you. Whatever you need, just ask."

"That's sweet. I'm so lucky to have you." His sister sniffled on the other end of the line, and Ty's throat started to close again. He cleared it quickly, needing to divert the conversation.

"Tell me about the guy," he said. "What does Martin do?"

"He's wonderful," she said. "Your classic grown-up Boy Scout. He's an attorney who fights on behalf of abused and at-risk kids. He owns his home and is this total model citizen. He's never even had a parking ticket. Isn't that crazy?"

Ty let out a breath he didn't realize he'd been holding. *Nothing like our father.*

"He sounds terrific," Ty said. "I can't wait to meet him."

"Great! Let me check my calendar, and I'll email you some dates that might work. We can go from there."

"Sounds perfect."

"So, how about you?" she said. "Any chance you'll take the plunge someday? Find a nice girl, settle down and have six kids and a dog and—"

"No." His response came out sharper than he meant it to, so he hurried to fill the awkward silence. "Not my thing."

He'd never be his father. That guy who destroyed families. It's why he avoided relationships and attachments like the plague.

He cleared his throat again.

"I'm happy for you, Anna," he said. "Tell me all about the wedding plans."

# Chapter Five

Ellie had every intention of flirting with Ty at her next video appointment. She'd picked out another sexy dress and even waxed her eyebrows.

But as was often the case, motherhood took center stage.

"Sweetie, when your teacher gives you a note to bring home to me, it's very important that you make sure I get it."

As she glanced into the rearview mirror, her son's lower lip quivered.

"I meant to," he said, his voice small and earnest. "But she kept talking about the dead lions, and I got scared."

"Dead lions?"

"She said there were dead lions and that if I didn't turn in the permission slip for the zoo field trip, I might not get to go."

"Deadlines," Ellie said, resisting the urge to smack her forehead. "The lions are all okay, sweetie. And I'm sorry you're missing the field trip."

"Me, too," he said. "But I'm glad I can go to work with you."

"So am I," Ellie said with only the tiniest twinge of

guilt. Her deepest, darkest, secret self wasn't thrilled by this unexpected schedule change. "I called Polly—you remember her, right?"

"The nurse who taught me how to make fart noises with my armpit?"

"Right," Ellie said. "A skill for which we are forever grateful. She's going to come pick you up at ten. Do you remember what that looks like on the clock?"

"The big hand is on the twelve, and the little hand is on the ten."

"Exactly. That's in thirty minutes." Ellie pulled into the parking lot and wondered which car was Ty's. Maybe the motorcycle? They were meeting at the main First Impressions office today, rather than Speak Up. Some sort of public presentation seminar had taken over the other building for the day.

"Grab your backpack, sweetie." Ellie held the car door open for Henry, then took his chubby little hand in hers.

Ty had been tied up with a client when Ellie had called to explain the scheduling snafu and to ask about changing the time.

"His schedule is pretty tight right now," the receptionist had told her. "Video is crazy hot these days, so he's booked months out."

"But my son—"

"No worries, hon. We've got lots of parents working here," the woman had said. "We know how it is. Just bring him with you. We can find a way to keep the little guy entertained."

Which is how Ellie found herself leading her six-year-old by the hand, hoping like hell he didn't ask her what was in the tote bag she carried.

*Well, sweetie, those are vibrators mommy planned to hold up for the camera...*

Um, no. While she certainly didn't lie to her son about

what she did for a living— *"Mommy sells grown-up things"* —
she wasn't about to advertise it.

"What an adorable little boy," the receptionist cooed as
Ellie led Henry past the front desk. "What's your name?"

"I'm Henry," he announced with pride as he shoved his
glasses up his freckled nose. "And I know all about how that
baby got in your tummy. Want me to tell you?"

Ellie grimaced and started to apologize, but the woman
just laughed. "You're such a smart young man," she said. "And
I'm sure your mommy is very proud of you for learning about
babies and grown-up things and about how some things are
best to only share with people when you know them really,
really well."

Ellie shot the woman a grateful look, earning herself a
smile in return. Henry furrowed his brow. "What? I didn't
show her my book. Or my penis."

"And I'm very glad about that." Ellie grabbed his hand
again. "Come on, baby. We're almost there."

She led Henry around a corner and down a narrow
flight of stairs to the video studio. The door was ajar, but she
knocked anyway.

"Ty? I'm so sorry I'm late. I had a little mix-up with
Henry's school schedule, and I tried to call, but—oh, crap!"

She spun Henry around by the arm at the same moment a
horrified Ty threw a jacket over his computer monitor.

A computer monitor that, if Ellie wasn't mistaken, showed
a very large image of a banana, a pair of kiwi fruit, and one
strategically-placed cock ring.

"Wow, hey," he said, stepping back from the monitor like
it was the most natural thing in the world to have a coat over
it. "This must be Henry?"

"I'm Henry," the boy confirmed, sticking out his hand.
"Why do you have fruit that looks like a penis?"

Ty didn't miss a beat. "Isn't that better than having a penis that looks like fruit?"

The boy seemed to mull that over and decide the stranger had a point.

"I'm Ty," he said. "I've heard a lot about you. Aren't you lucky, getting to come to work with mommy today?"

"He's getting picked up in half an hour." Ellie blew hair out of her eyes and shot Ty an apologetic look. "Thank you for understanding. We've had a crazy morning."

"Not a problem." Ty settled himself on a tall chair and splayed his hands over his knees. "I'm sure we can find a job around here for Mr. Henry. Maybe get him on the payroll so he can start helping with the light bill and paying his taxes like an upstanding citizen."

Henry giggled and adjusted his glasses. "I already have a job," he said. "I clean my room every night before I go to bed."

"And I'm sure you're terrific at it." Ty smiled at Ellie before directing his attention back to Henry. "Actually, I think you'd like some of the warm-up exercises I'd planned for your mom this morning. Would you like to help out with that?"

Henry's eyes went wide, and a flood of gratitude shot through Ellie's core. She glanced at Ty, relieved he didn't seem perturbed at all. He was calm and relaxed and totally unfazed by the unexpected juvenile guest. Not many guys could just roll with that.

She glanced back at the jacket-covered monitor and hesitated. "Uh, this exercise doesn't involve fruit, right?"

Ty shook his head and grinned. "Nope. We're going to stretch our face muscles so we're limbered up and animated for the camera."

"You can stretch your face?" Henry was in awe.

"Yep," Ty said. "Actors, like the ones you see on TV, do it all the time. Want to give it a shot?"

Ellie nodded, but Henry's response was more enthusiastic.

"Yes! Face exercising sounds like a good job. What do I hafta do?"

"The first one is called lion," Ty explained, and her boy's eyes widened in wonder.

"Like an alive lion? Not a dead one?"

"Not a dead one," Ty confirmed.

Henry smiled, relief evident on his freckled face. "The kids on the field trip are seeing dead ones, so this is way better."

Ellie thought about correcting him, but Ty was already off and running with the exercise. "Okay, so the idea is that you make your face like a lion's face. You want to make everything as big as possible. Your eyes and your mouth and your cheeks—kind of like a lion's mane. You think you can do that?"

"Yeah!" Henry grinned. "Do I get to rawr?"

"Definitely." Ty looked at Ellie. "You're doing this, too."

"Oh." She touched a hand to her collarbone, suddenly self-conscious. "Are you sure I need to—"

"Yep." He grinned. "I picked this warm-up just for you. It's all about letting go of the fear of looking silly and making sure your features are animated. It's a good exercise, I promise."

"Okay," Ellie agreed, more for Henry's sake than for Ty's. "I'm ready."

"On three," Ty said. "One, two, three—lion!"

Ty boggled his eyes and opened his mouth as wide as possible. He put his hands up like claws and let out a loud, low roar that sent Henry into peals of laughter.

"Rawr!" the little boy yelled, his mouth open wide and his eyes sparkling with joy.

"Rawr!" Ellie yelled back, lifting her own manicured claws in her best lion impression.

"Your mom's got this nailed," Ty told Henry. "I think she's had practice being a wildcat."

The flush shot all the way from Ellie's face to her fingertips, even though Ty didn't crack a smile or look at her. He was still focused on coaching Henry with a gentle patience that made Ellie's ovaries ache. How did Ty get so good at this? And why was it affecting her so much, the sight of her son with a man besides her brother?

*Down, girl. He's entertaining him, not auditioning for the role of stepdad.*

"You did an awesome job with that one, little man," Ty continued. "The next one is called fish. What do you think a fish looks like?"

Henry frowned in concentration then glanced at Ellie. "Wet?"

"Sure, but we're not going to get wet today."

Ellie commanded herself not to blush this time, though she wasn't terribly successful. She said a silent prayer of thanks Ty didn't look at her.

"Fish scrunch their faces up tight," Ty explained. "Their eyes, their mouths, their cheeks—it's pretty much the opposite of lion. Do you think you can do that?"

"Yeah!" Henry grinned. "One, two, three—fish!"

They all squished their faces up tight. Ellie squinted her eyes to tiny slits and scrunched her mouth up small. Not an easy feat when she was laughing at the funny expressions from Ty and Henry. God, she felt silly.

Silly and grateful. There was a tingle in the center of her belly that radiated all the way to her fingertips and toes.

"Nice job, man!" Ty held out a hand to high-five Henry, and the boy reached up to smack the massive palm with his small one.

"You, too!" Henry said. "You're a good fish."

"That'll come in handy if the video producer thing doesn't work out." Ty smiled at Ellie, and her ovaries twitched again. "How's your face? Are you nice and limbered up?"

She grinned. "I'm not sure what a limbered up face feels

like, but you definitely gave my smile muscles a workout."

"Excellent." Ty grinned. "Next, we can try—"

"I'm so sorry I'm late!"

Polly hustled in, her long gray braid sliding over one shoulder as she stooped to wrap Henry in a big hug. "Hey, big guy! You ready to go?"

"You're not late at all," Ellie assured her. "Thanks so much for coming. I owe you big time for this."

"Not a problem." Polly grinned. "Henry and I have big plans today, don't we?"

"Yeah!" Henry beamed and picked up his backpack. "Polly said next time we hung out we'd make a Batman costume."

Polly smiled and glanced at Ellie. "I hope that's okay. My nephew outgrew the black unitard he used five or six Halloweens ago, and I found some kid-size paintball armor at the thrift store for a dollar."

"That sounds wonderful." Ellie fumbled into her purse. "Here, let me grab some cash for supplies."

"Nah, this is just for fun." She smiled down at Henry. "Shall we get moving?"

"Uh-huh." Henry turned to Ty and stretched out his small hand. "It was very nice to meet you, Mr. Ty."

Ty grinned and shook the boy's hand with a professional solemnity that made Ellie's heart clench. "You, too, Mr. Henry."

Henry giggled and turned to Ellie. "Bye, Mommy."

"Bye, baby!" She knelt down and wrapped her arms around him, breathing in his sweet little-boy smell. "I love you."

"Love you, too!" Henry squeezed back then wriggled out of her arms and tore off toward the door. *Na-na-na-na-na-na-na-na-Batman!*

Ellie stood up and smiled at Polly. "Thanks again," she

said. "I'll text you when I'm done here. It shouldn't be more than a few hours."

"Take your time." Polly waved a hand then tossed her gray braid over one shoulder. "We've got plenty to keep us busy. Go have lunch or go for a bike ride or something."

Ellie smiled, grateful for the help. She'd watched Henry like a hawk the whole time he'd battled cancer, barely leaving his side to use the restroom. Now that he was in the clear, it was nice for them to have some breathing room now and then.

"You're the best," Ellie said. "Have fun, you two."

She waved as her son scampered down the hall with Polly on his heels, the older woman hustling to catch up when Henry stumbled a little on the carpet. He righted himself quickly, barely missing a note in his Batman song.

Ellie turned back to Ty. "Thanks so much for that. For being so cool with my kid." She leaned against his desk, more relaxed now than she'd been thirty minutes ago. "I know you weren't expecting to have to entertain a six-year-old today."

Ty shot a grimace at the jacket-covered computer. "Admittedly the appointment got off to a slightly different start than I expected, but that was fun. You have a great kid."

"I do, don't I?" She smiled. "I always wonder if people say that to all parents. Even when their kids are real assholes."

"If your kid were an asshole, I can promise you I would have found someplace else for him to hang out for the last half hour. Preferably a closet or something."

Ellie laughed as he pulled his jacket off the monitor then hung it neatly on a hook by the door. The screensaver had kicked in, but Ellie was still curious about the image she'd seen.

"You must have had a plan for today," she said. "Judging from what I saw on that screen."

He looked startled for a second, and Ellie wondered

if she'd just stuck her foot in her mouth. "I mean, I assume that was something for Madame Butterfly. Not that there's anything wrong with looking at porn—"

Ty's booming laugh halted her ridiculous flow of words, and Ellie shut her mouth.

"If I were surfing porn, I definitely wouldn't be checking out pictures of cock rings and fruit," he said.

"What *would* you be looking at?" she asked.

*Oh, hell. I said that out loud.* Ellie licked her lips, not sure whether to hide under the desk or run from the room.

*What was I thinking?*

She stared at Ty, heart thudding in her ears as she answered her own question.

*I was thinking that I want to seduce him. I'm out of practice, but maybe this is how it starts.*

"Are you asking about my turn-ons?" His eyes held hers, dark and molten and daring. "You want to know what gets me hot?"

Her heart skidded to a halt, ramming itself against her rib cage. *Is he flirting with me? Oh. My. God. What do I do?*

"Yes," she said, eyes locked with his as her pulse thudded in her head. "I guess I am. What gets you hot, Ty?"

# Chapter Six

Ty's heartbeat thrummed hard as he met those sea-blue eyes with his best effort not to blink. Or gawk. Or bend her over his desk and hike up that dress and—

"You're asking what turns me on?" he asked slowly.

Did she mean it? With his luck, he'd misheard her, and she'd asked for directions to the nearest library.

But the heat in her eyes suggested otherwise. He had a hunch the question had nothing to do with her job.

She wanted to know what got him hot.

Now *that* was a turn-on.

Ellie eased away from the desk. She'd been leaning against it, but now she stepped closer. Her cheeks were flushed, and her hands shook. That didn't stop her from edging into his space.

"Yes," she said. "You've seen my product demos. You've looked at my website. Even without all that, I imagine you have your own cache of sexual experiences to draw from."

Ty swallowed hard, fighting the instinct to reach for her. "Maybe one or two."

"I'm curious." Her voice was whispery now, her lips scant inches from his. "What gets your blood humming? What makes you breathe a little faster?"

*You,* his brain screamed.

He swallowed again. "Ellie."

She smiled. Did she know that was the answer to her question?

Inches separated them now. The floral notes of her perfume filled his senses.

He palmed the curve of her waist, pulling her against him more roughly than he intended.

But Ellie came willingly, molding her body against his like this was the plan all along. She gave a soft little gasp and tipped her head back, offering those delectable lips. His whole body howled with the urge to kiss her. Sliding his free hand into the hair at the nape of her neck, he drew her nearer.

Then he claimed her mouth.

*So sweet.*

Ellie moaned then grabbed his ass to pull him snug against her heat. Everything in his brain tilted, reorienting itself to this version of Ellie. The Ellie grinding rough against him while her lips parted softly against his.

*So soft.*

He deepened the kiss, exploring her mouth as his fingers threaded into her hair. Had any woman ever made him this dizzy, this crazy with need? Hell, no. It was all her. Only her.

He kissed her harder, too mind-wacked to care that he was losing all sense of reality. She responded in kind, arching against him, kissing him with startling intensity. Her lips tasted sweet like strawberries, and he wondered if it was her lip gloss or just Ellie.

He inched one hand up from her waist, aching to skim the tips of his fingers against the underside of her breast. Braced for her to nudge his hand back down, he was still startled when she broke the kiss and grabbed the back of his hand.

"Touch me," she gasped, pushing his hand over her breast. "Please, Ty."

*Sweet mother of—*

He obeyed—what kind of fucking idiot wouldn't?—squeezing all that delicious softness as he grazed his thumb over one nipple. She moaned in response and pressed closer. Touching her like this sent his brain spinning again, whirling in a downward spiral that smacked his heart on the way through his core. Did that even make sense? He was losing it, his grip on reality slipping from his fingers as they slid through her hair.

He took one step back and bumped the edge of his desk, pulling her with him. She came willingly, and it killed him to know she wanted this, too. That she felt even a fraction of the desire that bubbled in his chest. How was it possible for a woman to be this sweet and this mind-bendingly sexy all at once?

He didn't know, but it made him fucking insane.

Ty kissed her deeper, wanting more of it. Wanting all of her. Wanting to push his free hand under the hem of her dress, hiking it up until he—

"Hey, guys, I was wondering if I could steal Ellie for—oh."

Ty jumped back, knocking the tape dispenser off the corner of his desk and leaving Ellie standing there with just-kissed lips and a baffled look on her face.

"Miriam," Ty said, clearing her throat. "I was just—we were just—"

"Kissing," Ellie said, taking a small step back. "We were kissing."

Miriam grinned and shifted a stack of papers from one arm to the other. "Is that what that was?" She smirked at Ty. "For a second I thought you might try to tell me you were getting something out of her eye."

"I might have if I'd thought of it," he muttered.

Miriam laughed and waved a dismissive hand. "Don't bother. Nice lip gloss, by the way."

Ty swiped the back of his hand over his mouth and tried to recall if there were any company rules prohibiting fraternization between clients and company execs. As his gaze landed on the boss's pregnant belly, he figured maybe not.

Seeming to read his mind, Miriam laughed again. "Hey, remember that time I hooked up with a client and we got married and lived happily ever after?" She smirked and rested a hand on her baby bump. "Or when my business partner nailed the guy who hired her to remake his professional brand, and now they have a beautiful baby boy?"

Ellie licked her lips, giving Ty the urge to claim them again. "How's Holly doing, anyway?" she asked. "Is Evan's colic better?"

Ty blinked and tried to remember how First Impressions' other owner had met her husband. Definitely through work. He couldn't recall details, but at this point, he wasn't sure he remembered his own name.

"That baby is such a sweetie," Miriam said to Ellie. "Thanks again for all the tips you gave them."

"No problem. Henry had trouble with colic, so I learned a lot the hard way."

Ty rubbed a hand over the back of his neck and tried to figure out how he'd gone from groping a beautiful woman to discussing childhood flatulence in under a minute. He took a deep breath as something twisted hard at his gut. He didn't hate the kid talk. It wasn't that. There was actually something sweet and beautiful about Ellie's domestic side. About how kind and nurturing she was with family. It was one of the things he loved about her.

*Love.*

No.

That wasn't in the cards for him. Not even close. He damn well knew better than to start wanting something like that for himself. He was Johnny Hendrix's son. He was a guy whose lone parental figure once took him to the mall and forgot him there, only remembering hours after stores closed that he'd left his six-year-old alone.

*That's what you know. How you were raised. And it's why you have to steer clear—so you don't fuck things up for this sweet mother and her kid.*

Ty raked a hand down his face and took a step back. At least he tried to. He only managed to knock his stapler on the ground. It landed atop the tape dispenser, making a loud clatter.

Ellie raised one eyebrow at him. "You need to get that?"

"Yeah," he said. He stepped away from her and picked up the office supplies, then moved to the other side of the desk to put some more space between them. He tried to put his focus back on work, reaching out to jiggle the mouse and wake up his computer.

Bad idea.

The fruit and cock ring image blared back at him like a tortuous sexual taunt.

"Well." Miriam cleared her throat. "I just stopped by to see if Ellie's free for lunch, but I should probably let you two get back to work."

"Work," Ty repeated, giving a vigorous nod. "Yes. That's what we should do. Ready to work, Ellie?"

He glanced up to see Ellie standing there, confused.

But he needed to keep some distance between them. A desk between them, at least.

"Yes," she said, finding her voice at last. "Yes to lunch, and yes to working. Yes to all of it."

She held his gaze for a moment, communicating a message Ty heard loud and clear.

*I want you, jerk. And this isn't over yet.*

Ty stared back, wishing there were some way for her to read his mind.

*Trust me, babe. I'm the last thing you want.*

• • •

Ellie forked up a bite of kale salad and stole a covert glance at her sister-in-law, wondering if Miriam planned to bring up the lip-lock with Ty.

She didn't have to wonder long.

"So apparently Plan Seduce-the-Videographer is off to a good start," Miriam said, grinning as she reached across the table to spear a cucumber in Ellie's salad. Ellie didn't mind, since she'd been stealing Miriam's croutons. "Sorry about walking in on you like that," Miriam added. "It looked like things were just getting good."

"It's fine," Ellie assured her, even though it kinda wasn't. After Miriam left, Ty had behaved like the consummate professional. He'd been respectful, composed, and dignified. She might have been grateful if it weren't for the fact that she wanted to hump his leg like a feral poodle.

Shaking her head to rid her brain of the dog image, she met her sister-in-law's eyes with an uncertain shrug. "I can't tell if he's interested in me," she admitted.

Miriam quirked an eyebrow at her. "His hand on your boob and his tongue in your mouth weren't an indication?"

"I kissed *him*," Ellie pointed out. "Maybe he was just being polite."

"Honey, the man was ten seconds from boosting you onto his desk and devouring you like a cream puff. I don't think he was being polite."

"Then why did he back off the way he did?"

Miriam set her fork down, a flicker of sympathy in her

eyes. "Uh, maybe because having his business partner watch isn't his idea of a turn-on?"

"No, I mean afterward," Ellie said. "He could have kissed me again. Instead, he got right down to business. Started pulling up spreadsheets and everything." She gave a desperate little laugh as she stabbed a tomato harder than necessary. "For crying out loud, he shook my hand when I left."

"Hmm." Miriam seemed to consider that as she picked up her fork again and swirled a hunk of romaine in a puddle of dressing. "I'm trying to remember the conversation. We started talking about babies, right?"

"Right," Ellie said, though, truth be told, she wasn't sure. Her brain had been a little fuzzy for the first few minutes after Miriam's entrance.

"So maybe the whole kid thing is awkward for him," Miriam suggested. "I asked him once if he has any nieces or nephews, and he looked at me like I'd asked if he's into amputee porn."

"Yeah," Ellie mused, considering the nervousness on Ty's face when she'd first walked in with Henry. She'd chalked it up to the faux pas with the sexy fruit on his computer screen, but maybe there was more to it. "I don't get the sense he's been around kids much."

"He almost never talks about family," Miriam said. "In the six years I've known him, I've never once met any siblings or parents or anything. I don't even know for sure if he *has* family."

Ellie nodded, remembering Ty's comments about his father.

*I had an asshole dad of my own.*

If Ty didn't often talk about family, maybe it meant something that he'd shared that with her. Maybe she owed it to him to protect that trust.

"I suppose the baby stuff might have thrown him for a loop," Ellie acknowledged. "That, and having Henry with us for the first part of the morning."

"He met Henry?"

"Yeah." Ellie smiled at the memory of how gracious Ty had been. How sweet and funny and welcoming. "He was actually pretty amazing with him."

"That's great!" Miriam looked thoughtful. "And the fact that he kissed you after meeting your kid means he's not totally wigged out by the single mom thing."

"I suppose," Ellie said, trying not to feel too hopeful. "Maybe I just need to get him alone and talk about something besides colic and babysitters."

"Sex toys seem like a more promising subject." Miriam forked up a bite of salad and slid it into her mouth. As she chewed, her eyes went wide the way they always did when she had a big idea, but manners kept her from blurting it out with a mouthful of romaine. Her sister-in-law chewed at warp speed.

"I know!" Miriam said as soon as she swallowed. "Isn't this the boys' weekend coming up?"

"You mean Jason and Henry's camping trip?"

"Yes! They're going to Suttle Lake. That's four hours away, right?"

"Right," Ellie said slowly, not sure where this conversation was headed.

"What were you planning to do while they're gone?"

"Clean the house, pay my quarterly taxes, and binge-watch old episodes of *Parks and Rec* on Netflix."

Miriam shook her head. "No, this is perfect!"

"What's perfect?"

"This is your chance to seduce Ty," she said. "Invite him over to your house for dinner. Light some candles, put on a sexy dress, maybe make some sort of special dinner with aphrodisiac properties…"

"Does lasagna have aphrodisiac properties?"

Miriam laughed. "I've had your lasagna. If I hadn't

already been sleeping with your brother, I totally would have jumped you."

"Thank you."

Miriam grinned. "All I'm saying is that a romantic dinner at your place might lead to something. Especially with your kid and your brother gone for the weekend."

She gave an exaggerated eyebrow wiggle, which made Ellie laugh.

But it made her think, too. Made her imagine how an intimate dinner date at her place might unfold. She pictured Ty with his shirt sleeves rolled up, candlelight flickering in his eyes as he shoved the dishes aside, boosted her up on the table, and—

"Earth to Ellie…"

She blinked and looked back at Miriam. "I think it's a great idea."

"Yeah?" Miriam grinned. "I've been known to have a few of them from time to time."

Ellie glanced at her watch. "Maybe I even have time to hit that little consignment shop around the corner to find a sexy dress."

"At the rate you're trotting out the sexy dresses, the man's going to think you don't wear anything else."

Ellie frowned. "You think it's too much?"

"No, I think it's fine. I like seeing you come out of your shell a bit. Embracing your inner sex goddess somewhere besides online forums."

"It has been fun," she admitted, poking at a questionable slice of celery. "God, if Chuck saw me now. He'd die."

"You didn't dress sexy for your ex?"

She shrugged and glanced down at her plate. "Not often. I tried a few times, but he didn't really respond. Well, there was one time I put on a little black negligee and surprised him in the living room."

"Did he jump you on the coffee table?" Miriam smiled and dabbed the corner of her mouth with a napkin.

"He asked me to move so he could see the TV."

"Ouch." Miriam glared. "Ass-hat."

"Pretty much." Ellie shrugged to let her know it wasn't still bothering her, even though it was. "Eventually, I stopped trying."

Miriam reached across the table and squeezed her hand. "Well, I can guarantee you Ty is noticing."

A smile spread across Ellie's face. She took a bite of salad to cover it, but it was impossible to hide the giddiness she felt at the thought of seducing Ty.

"Well, okay, then," she said. "It's time to take things to the next level."

• • •

Ty's phone was at the other end of the house that night when he heard it chime with the ringtone he'd assigned to Ellie Sanders. He sprinted for it, stubbing his toe on the baseboard as he rounded the corner from the hall.

"Stupid dog-reaming jackwagon—" He skidded to a halt in front of the entry table that held his phone.

It also held the only photograph he owned of his late grandmother, and he waited for his chest to stop squeezing before he answered the call.

"Hey, Ellie."

"Ty! You sound out of breath. Did I interrupt something?"

"No, definitely not. I was just…working out."

He wanted to punch himself for lying to her, and for no reason at all. Jesus. Did pathological lying run in families? It must. He sat down on the sofa with the phone in one hand.

"Okay, good." Ellie took a breath on the other end of the line. "I was wondering if you'd like to come over for dinner."

"Dinner?" He lowered his foot to the floor and focused on not being an asshole. "I...um...sure. What's the occasion?"

"Oh, no occasion." She sounded breezy and casual, and Ty had the feeling she was forcing it a little. "Henry's out of town with my brother, so I thought it might be nice to have you over. You know, as a thank you for all the video work you're doing for me."

"You've already thanked me by doing all that voiceover work." He wished he hadn't said that.

"I know, but I wanted the chance to visit with you outside of work," she said.

Ty's heart lurched, but he punched it back down into the hollow center of his chest. "That would be nice," he said carefully.

"Some one-on-one time would be a great networking opportunity, plus it would be great to interface about professional strategy outside the confines of work," she added.

Ty frowned, trying to figure out why she sounded like she was reading from the handbook of bad business jargon. Was this a date or a business dinner? Which did he want?

*You want to be professional,* he reminded himself. *You can't get involved, remember?*

He cleared his throat. "Dinner sounds great," he said. "Name the time and the place, and I'll be there."

"Great!" The enthusiasm in that single syllable gave Ty a fresh jolt of excitement, and he ordered himself to knock it off. To keep his damn emotions out of the equation.

Ellie rattled off the date and an address, chattering a bit longer about action items and best practices until Ty had no idea if she was talking dirty or what.

But the one thing he did know was that he couldn't wait to see her.

And that scared the hell out of him.

# Chapter Seven

Ty made his way up the sidewalk leading to Ellie's duplex, glancing once at his watch to make sure he wasn't too early. Nope, right on time.

He clutched a bouquet of daisies in one hand and a bottle of wine in the other, hoping like hell he wasn't way off base with either one. He still wasn't sure if this was a business meeting or a date.

A date would be a dumb I idea. Didn't keep him from wanting it, though.

As he stood on the doorstep steeling himself to knock, nervous vibes coursed through him like an electric current. His palms itched, and he couldn't stop his idiot heart from doing its best impression of a kettledrum. *It's just dinner,* he reminded himself. *Dinner with a business associate.*

*A business associate who kissed you senseless,* added another voice from the deeper recesses of his brain. *A business associate with breasts that fit so perfectly in your palm it's like they were meant to go together. Like chocolate and peanut butter. Or chips and salsa. Or Madame Butterfly's Strawberry*

*Tingle Gel and—*

"Not helpful," Ty muttered as he lifted his hand to knock.

The door flew open, and Ty had an instant view of the aforementioned breasts. They were displayed in shocking detail under a soaking wet T-shirt dress. The thin cotton was plastered to her skin, leaving nothing to the imagination as Ellie's nipples jutted toward him like party invitations.

He blinked, pretty sure he was imagining things.

Nope. Ellie was standing in her doorway wearing a drenched pink cotton dress that clung to her like Saran Wrap. Ty could see everything. Seriously—*everything*. He might have reached for her right then if it weren't for the panic on her face.

"Ty." She peeled the sopping cotton away from her breasts, but the stubborn garment sucked right back into place. She gave a small growl of frustration. "Fuck!"

"Ellie? What's wrong? Are you okay?"

His desire switch flipped off, and his brain flooded with concern. Was she hurt? The urge to protect her hit him with a fierceness that pulled the breath from his lungs.

She shook her head and spit out a damp hank of hair. "The pipe under my kitchen sink just blew up," she said. "I tried to stop the water, but it's spurting everywhere like a fucking geyser, and now my kitchen is flooding and I'm freaking out."

"Show me." Not waiting for an invitation, he pushed through the door. Ellie stepped back, then turned and hurried ahead into a tidy little kitchen with slate counters. Well, it had been tidy. The puddles of water on the gray tile floor weren't so tidy. Beneath the sink, a cupboard gaped open, water spewing from it like a fire hydrant.

Ty dove for it, fumbling through the geyser for the shutoff valve. His fingers found the knob, slipping once before he grabbed hold of it. He twisted hard, but it wouldn't budge.

"God, it's stuck," he grunted.

"I know! I've been fighting with it for five minutes."

"Come on, you infected cock-felcher," Ty muttered, throwing every ounce of strength into moving the knob. The rusty handle began to turn, slowing the streams of water. "That's it, you piss-bathing son of a–" The flow petered out to a slow gush, then a dribble.

He glanced behind him to see Ellie looking bemused.

"Apparently, I needed to curse at it," she said. "Who knew?"

Ty grunted then ducked back under the sink for a closer look. The water wasn't gushing anymore, but it still seeped from several spots. He peered at the pipe, unsurprised to see a cluster of small pinholes. "Corrosion," he muttered. "Could be chloramines, or maybe your water heater is old. That'll cause pinhole leaks like this."

"I know a new water heater is on the list," Ellie admitted. "My brother bought this duplex as a fixer-upper. We've been renting it at a discount while he chips away at repairs."

"This should probably be your next one." Ty sat up and wiped his hands on his jeans.

"No kidding." She bit her lip. "Is there any way to patch things up until he comes home Sunday?"

Ty leaned back on his heels and scratched his chin with a damp hand. "I don't suppose you have any epoxy."

She frowned. "I don't think so. We keep all the home repair stuff in the other duplex next door. It's vacant right now while Jason fixes it up for the next renter."

"Any chance you have a spare key?"

Ellie shook her head. "Normally I'd run down the street and grab it from Miriam, but she's out of town."

"Let me see what I've got in my toolbox."

Ellie stared at him. "You brought a toolbox to dinner?"

Ty nodded as he got to his feet. "I always keep one in my truck, just in case."

"I think I might love you."

She meant it as a joke, but the words sent a pleasant throb through his chest. He turned away, not wanting her to read anything on his face. He hurried back through the living room and out the front door, wondering if he should call Home Depot. But it was already late, and the odds of getting all the way there before closing seemed slim.

He'd have to make do. He grabbed the toolbox and hustled back to the house, heading straight for the kitchen this time without knocking. Ellie was on her hands and knees mopping at the water with a pile of old towels, and Ty felt like an asshole for noticing the curve of her backside.

*God, you're a pig. What kind of asshole ogles a woman in distress?*

Ty took a deep breath and set the toolbox on the counter. Ellie looked up as he opened the lid and began rummaging through the contents.

"I'm so sorry, Ty," she said.

His heart twisted a little at the unhappy note in her voice. "It's not a problem," he said, meaning it. "I'm glad to help."

"I swear I didn't invite you here to be my plumber."

"Oh, you'll still need a plumber." He located a stray C-clamp and kept digging, hoping to find an old tube of epoxy. "But I should at least be able to plug your hole."

Silence met him in response, and Ty slowly replayed his words. *Hell.* He glanced at Ellie to see she wore a strange expression.

"Um, right." She swiped a damp hank of hair off a cheek that seemed pinker than normal. "Plugging my hole would be—helpful."

Ty's dick twinged. *No. I'm not sporting wood in the middle of her kitchen.*

He dug through the toolbox some more, annoyed not to see any epoxy or pipe repair clamps or Teflon tape or anything else he might need. How the hell was he supposed to help her? Something inside him desperately wanted to, *needed* to be the guy to make things okay for her.

He glanced back at Ellie, who was using a Batman beach towel to mop up a small lake next to the fridge. "Any chance you have a patch kit?" he asked.

"You mean for pipes?"

"I was thinking more like the kind you'd use for a rubber raft or an air mattress or something."

She frowned, looking dubious as she shoved a damp towel aside and reached for a dry one. "I don't think so. I had water wings for Henry when he was little, but those are probably long gone."

"Or just a stray piece of rubber will do," he said. "An old bike inner tube or garden hose or something?"

Ellie bit her lip. "I can look around the house." She stopped sponging at the water and sat back on her heels. "Jason and Henry took their bikes camping, and my bike is in the shop getting a tune-up. My patch kit is still in my seat bag."

Ty glanced back at the pipe and frowned. Hesitating, he glanced back at Ellie. Hell.

"Okay. Don't judge." Keeping his eyes off her, he slid his hand into his back pocket and pulled out his wallet. "I'm pretty sure this will work," he said as he slid out the condom and tore open the foil packet.

He dared a glance at her then, noticing the stunned look on her face. Was she upset?

"Oh." Ellie stared at him, cheeks going from soft pink to a hue on the edge of crimson. "Well, that's one way to do it."

Ty shoved the wrapper in the trash and unrolled the condom. "It's the right size, and durable and—"

"Right. Yes, of course." Ellie sat back on her heels, her dress still plastered to her breasts. She plucked at the wet fabric, driving him mindless with the peripheral view of her hand reaching for her breasts again and again.

Ty focused on his work.

"You know, you shouldn't store condoms in your wallet," she said. "There's this whole big article about it on the Madame Butterfly website. Apparently, if you leave them in there for a long time, the friction from repeatedly opening and closing the wallet will degrade the latex and make holes in the condom."

"It's only been in there an hour," he said slowly. "So, it should be safe."

Ellie stared at him, and he waited for the words to register.

She smiled. "Oh. *Oh.*" The smile got wider, and she plucked at her damp dress again. "I see."

Ty nodded, then turned back to the task at hand. He tried not to think of how he'd imagined using the damn condom when he put it there before leaving for dinner, but how could he not? Ellie was just a few feet away, lush and wet and so fuckable that his brain had short-circuited.

He yanked a utility knife out of his back pocket and began trimming the condom to size.

"What else do you need?" Ellie asked. "Um. For the repair, I mean."

"A couple blocks of wood would be great." Ty set the knife down and held up his hands. "Maybe about this thick and this long?"

Ellie stared, eyes fixed on his fingers and palms, then nodded. "I'll see what I can find."

She scrambled up, slipping once in a puddle. Ty reached out to catch her, but she was on her feet before he put his hands on her.

Dammit.

Part of him felt like a dick for not doing a better job helping her. Another part felt like a dick for ogling her. Either way, that was an awful lot of dick feelings.

*Jesus. Control yourself.*

He turned back to his work, needing to concentrate on Ellie's pipe so he wouldn't be so fixated on his own.

*You're such a pig. Just like your old man.*

Something crashed at the other end of the house, and Ty wondered if he should check on Ellie. "You okay?"

"Fine, fine," she called. "Just looking for that wood."

Ty swallowed hard and wondered if he should just call an after-hours plumber. That's what a better guy would do. A guy who'd stay focused on helping Ellie instead of thinking illicit thoughts about her. She deserved a hero, not a creeper. He muttered under his breath, curse words that seemed creative even for him.

"What's that?" she called.

"Nothing," he yelled back, wondering if lust had pickled his brain and made it seep into his eardrums. "If you have any thread sealing tape, can you grab that?"

It was unlikely, but he might as well ask. He pressed the condom over the pinprick holes in the pipe, doing his best to create a seal.

Footsteps alerted him to Ellie's return. She held out a pair of kid's building blocks—one red, one yellow—along with a spool of bright purple tape Ty recognized.

He squinted at it. "Is that the bondage tape you were using the other night?"

She nodded, embarrassed. "I know it's not exactly what you asked for, but I thought maybe it could work."

"It's worth a shot."

Ellie took a step back and Ty placed one block on each side of the condom-covered pipe.

"What are those for?" Ellie asked from behind him.

"It's to spread the pressure out," he said. "The pipe is already corroded, so we don't want it to collapse once I start tightening the C-clamp."

"I'm not sure what a C-clamp is, but it sounds like something I'd sell at one of my parties."

He snorted, appreciating her sense of humor. Plenty of women would be freaking out over a flooded kitchen and major plumbing damage, but not Ellie. She was taking it all in stride.

God, what a woman.

*Stop thinking about her.*

He slipped the metal piece into place and began spinning the slippery screw, fumbling to get it nice and tight without thinking words like "slippery screw" and "nice and tight" and pretty much anything else that might make him want to bend Ellie over the kitchen counter.

Which was pointless, really. He could open a dictionary at random and point to any word at all. *Aardvark. Kiwi. Valance.* Any of them made him want to put his hands all over Ellie Sanders.

Or maybe that was Ellie herself. She was standing close enough for Ty to see up her dress if he turned his head at all, so he concentrated hard on not doing that.

He turned the screw one last time then checked the clamp to make sure it was snug. Then he turned his attention to the spot where the pipe disappeared into the wall at the back of the cupboard. He frowned and touched a fingertip to the fitting.

"Damn."

"What's the matter?" Ellie asked.

Ty put his fingers around it and gave it a wiggle. "The nut is plenty tight, but it's still dripping for some reason," he muttered. "Can you hand me the tape?"

Ellie stooped down beside him and picked up the bondage tape. Placing it in his palm, she peered into the cupboard. "Oh. I see what you mean."

Her shoulder bumped his, and lust blasted through him again. There was so much of it surging through his veins that it was probably flooding his organs. His skin hummed with heat, and he thought about stabbing his utility knife straight into the pipe to start another geyser.

*Cold shower. Please.*

"I might need a hand getting this wrapped around the male end of the fitting."

"Whatever you need," Ellie said.

"Here, can you hold this?"

Ellie grabbed the pipe, and Ty concentrated on wrapping the purple tape around the threads, careful not to twist it or overlap it or throw it aside to reach for her.

"There," he said, spinning the nut back into place over the tape-covered threads. "That should do it."

They sat back and admired his handiwork.

"Unreal," Ellie said. "You did it."

"Yeah," Ty said, surprised by the swell of pride bubbling in his chest.

"You fixed my kitchen sink with a condom, bondage tape, and my son's building blocks."

Ty nodded and wiped his hands down the front of his jeans. "Should we post it to the do-it-yourself page on Home Depot's website?"

She laughed and brushed a damp clump of hair off her face. "Thank you so much, Ty. I don't know what I would have done without you."

"Probably gotten a lot wetter," he said.

The second he said it, he wanted to grab the words back and shove them down his throat.

*What the hell is wrong with you?*

But Ellie just laughed. "I don't think it would be possible."

She smiled again, eyes locked with his, those twin pools of blue shimmering with something familiar. His body buzzed with twin pulses of desire and affection as she sat beside him, damp and disheveled and so damn beautiful his heart turned to mush.

Her gaze dropped to his chest and she frowned. "Sorry about your shirt."

There was a wet patch over his heart. Maybe it really had melted. "It's fine," he said. "It's just water."

"Let me throw it in the dryer for you," she said.

Ellie scrambled to her feet before he could insist it wasn't necessary.

He stood up and shrugged out of his plaid button-down. "Thanks." He peeled off the white undershirt, too, folding both over his arm before handing them to her. "I appreciate it."

Ellie stared at his chest for a few beats. "Good Lord," she murmured. "How many hours in the gym does it take to look like that?"

Ty laughed, secretly flattered. "I have a lot of free time on my hands."

She seemed to shake herself a bit then, and her gaze lifted to his. "Sorry. I didn't mean to ogle you."

He took a deep breath, determined not to look away this time. "I've been ogling you in that wet dress for the last twenty minutes," he said. "It's a fair trade."

Ellie grinned up at him like he'd just offered her a glass of wine and a foot rub. "Then it sounds like we're on the same page."

Before he could say anything else, she turned and scurried down the hall.

*What just happened?*

"Let me see if I can find one of my brother's old shirts somewhere," she called from the other end of the house.

"I'm fine," he yelled back, then lowered his voice. "I probably need to cool off a bit anyway."

He thought he heard a bubble of laughter from down the hall, but that was all. There was a clang, followed by the sound of a clothes dryer starting up. Ty grabbed a dry towel from a stack on the counter and dropped to his knees to mop the puddle closest to the fridge. When he finished with that one, he set the wet towel in the sink and repeated the process with another puddle and another towel.

Once he had the floor reasonably tidy, he grabbed a dish towel off the counter and dried his hands. Feeling awkward standing shirtless in her kitchen, he turned and headed into the living room. He was most definitely not thinking about Ellie taking off her dress down the hall. That was none of his business.

*Get a grip, Hendrix.*

He stalked over to the couch and sat down hard, figuring he was least likely to get into trouble here. Maybe he should pour them each some of the wine he'd brought, but that might be weird. Too intimate to go digging through her cupboards for a corkscrew and glasses. He should probably just wait right here and try not to do anything stupid.

A sound from the hallway made Ty glance up. His jaw fell open as Ellie strolled toward him wearing a pink robe that tied at the waist. The silky fabric covered her arms and came almost to the floor. She was perfectly decent, probably more covered up than any of the other times they'd met.

But his head started to buzz as his gaze lingered at the deep V between her breasts. Was she wearing anything under that robe? Or would one little tug on that silky belt leave her standing naked in her living room?

"That feels better," Ellie said, rubbing a towel over her damp hair. She grinned at him then tossed the towel through an open door he guessed might be to the laundry room. She strode toward him, Ty's gaze clinging to her like static on a balloon.

He should strike up some casual banter, but the only thing swimming up through the murk in his brain was, *Are you naked under there?*

He couldn't say that. He hadn't said it, right? It was possible his tongue wasn't entirely under control.

"Music!" he blurted like an idiot. "We should turn on some music."

Ellie looked at him oddly then nodded. "Sure. My iPod is right there next to you. See if there's anything you like."

Ty tore his eyes off her and fumbled with the iPod. Metallica? Guns N' Roses? AC/DC?

"You like eighties metal?" he asked.

"I love it," she said as she eased onto the couch beside him, close enough for Ty to feel the warmth of her thigh through the silky robe.

He didn't know which he found sexier—that or her musical taste. A woman who liked to rock? That was ridiculously hot. Maybe hotter than a woman who sold sex toys for a living.

Christ. How was it possible for one woman to be so many things he found insanely attractive?

"Your shirt will be dry in just a few minutes," Ellie said. "I hope it's okay I threw my dress in there, too."

"Fine with me," he said. His voice sounded crackly, and he wondered what kind of a perv got turned on by the thought of his clothes tumbling around together with a gorgeous woman's dress.

"I know it's silly," she said. "I should have just put on another dress, but that one was perfect for the occasion."

Ty swallowed hard, wondering why there was no air in the room.

Ellie's words echoed in his head, sinking through the layers. He looked up at her, not sure what she meant. "Perfect for the occasion," he repeated as his brain tried desperately to keep up with the conversation. "What's the occasion?"

She didn't answer right away but just stared at him like she was choosing her next words carefully, weighing them in her palms like dumbbells. Then she smiled, and something clenched deep in his gut.

"The occasion," she said, "is I planned to seduce you."

# Chapter Eight

Ellie held Ty's gaze, fighting with everything she had not to blink or look away or hide under the couch like a big, fat chicken as she waited for his response to her bold declaration.

*I planned to seduce you.*

It was true, but so far nothing about this evening had gone right.

Ty stared like she'd just announced her intent to tie him to the bed and cover him with motor oil. She couldn't tell from his expression whether he found that intriguing or horrifying.

She licked her lips, desperate to fill the awkward silence. "I know things got off to kind of a weird start," she said. "I was planning to greet you at the door and hand you a glass of wine and make casual small talk about this article I just read about the differences between male and female orgasms, but them my kitchen flooded and now you're sitting here shirtless on my couch and this is totally not how I saw this going, but I thought maybe—"

"Okay." Ty set the iPod beside him on the sofa and reached out like he was going to take her hand. Then he stopped, resting both huge palms on his knees. "Just so we're clear, are you just looking for a hookup, or were you thinking of something more, uh…" He stopped, frowning, and Ellie got the sense he was searching for a polite way to finish the same thought that had been ricocheting through her brain all week.

"I'm not after a boyfriend or husband or stepdad or anything remotely like that," she said. "Just sex." She tucked a still-damp lock of hair behind one ear and held his gaze with hers. "And I thought maybe you might be on the same page."

In all her fantasies, she'd sounded like a cool and composed modern woman. Not like a crazy lady sitting here in her bathrobe with wet hair and a goose egg on her forehead from where she'd whacked herself on the cupboard trying to fix her own damn pipe.

Ty's face told her maybe he wasn't too concerned with her lack of finesse. Maybe he wanted the same thing she did.

"I want you," he said. "But—"

Ellie winced. "I knew there'd be a but." She wished the rejection didn't sting this much. "How about we just pretend this never happened?"

"Ellie." Ty put a hand on her leg, and she opened her eyes to stare at it. The sight of that massive palm cupping her satin-covered knee sent a full-body shiver rippling through her. His thumb flicked the fabric aside to reveal a bare swath of skin. Sliding his palm to the side, he claimed that flesh, too.

Something about the deliberateness of his movements braced her to meet his eyes again. "We're totally on the same page here," he said in a voice so low she had to lean closer to hear. "I want you. I *really* want you. I figured the condom in my wallet clued you in."

"Right." Ellie nodded, still fixated on his fingertips making slow circles over her calf. She wondered if it was possible to have an orgasm just from a man touching her leg. At the rate he was going, it seemed likely.

"But I just used my only condom to fix your pipe," he said. "So, unless you have a stash, we might need to call a halt to things for now."

"Oh." Relief sluiced through her, and she found herself grinning. "No problem there! I have tons of condoms. Thousands."

"Uh—"

"Ribbed and flavored and extra-large and—" She stopped talking as his eyebrow lifted. Oh. "I don't mean because I'm a raging hussy or anything like that."

Ty smiled. "Hussy," he repeated. "That was my grandmother's favorite word."

A spark of sadness lit his eyes for an instant, but he spoke again before Ellie asked about it. "I would never think of you that way," he said. His palm clenched tighter around her knee as his fingertips stroked her calf. "And I'd never judge you for knowing what you want."

Ellie laughed, wondering if she should just shut the hell up and kiss him before she killed the mojo completely. "I'll be right back."

She scrambled off the couch and raced down the hallway to her bedroom. She kept her Madame Butterfly stash in a locked cabinet to prevent Henry from stumbling onto it and mistaking the Tickle Me Pretty for a cat toy or something like that. She fumbled into the back of her jewelry box for the key, then jammed it into the cabinet lock and yanked the door open. As she pawed through her big box of condoms, it occurred to her how long it had been since she'd done this. Where did she even start? There were so many options.

*Lubricated condoms, lambskin, pineapple flavored, condoms dotted with pleasure nubs—*

She grabbed the biggest handful she could manage and scrambled back to the living room, spilling condoms as she hustled back to where Ty sat waiting on the couch with a funny little smile on his face. His gaze moved to her hand as she opened her fist and dropped at least two dozen packets onto the sofa beside him.

He stared at them for a moment, then looked up with a hint of alarm. "I'm flattered by your expectations, but I should probably let you know that I have to be back at work by Monday."

Ellie shifted her weight from one foot to the other, conscious of her robe slipping open in front. She reached up to pull it closed, then stopped herself. If the next few minutes went the way she hoped, covering up was beside the point.

"I grabbed some of everything," she said. "I wasn't sure what you liked."

"This." Ty reached up and pulled her in to straddle his lap. She let her legs fall open as she came to rest with him centered between her thighs. Her robe parted, slipping off one shoulder. She started to reach for it, but Ty caught both of her hands in one of his.

"So beautiful," he said, planting a kiss on her bare shoulder. He was miles away from her breast, but somehow that simple, nearly-chaste kiss sent fiery rockets of lust to every nerve ending in her body.

Ellie shivered, conscious of the bulge of denim pressing into the junction of her legs. She wondered if she should have paid more attention to the condoms she'd grabbed. It was clear they'd be needing the extra-large.

Before she could blurt something awkward about that, Ty's mouth found hers.

Then he was kissing her with a delicious heat that made her toes curl into the couch cushion. She dragged her hands down his bare chest, thrilled to discover he felt even better than he looked. The muscles were taut and silky, with the faintest dusting of hair in the center. She traced a fingertip over the Johnny Cash tattoo, wondering about the story there.

Then she forgot all about it as he deepened the kiss, sliding his hands up her sides to graze the edges of her breasts through heated satin. Ellie gasped and ground against him, conscious of the delicious friction at her core.

Ty seemed to read her thoughts because his fingers found the edges of her robe and gave a soft tug. Ellie sucked in a breath as the robe fell open, and he shoved it the rest of the way off her shoulders.

She held her breath, waiting. How long had it been since any man had seen her like this?

Ty broke the kiss and smiled up at her. "You're beautiful, Ellie."

He was looking at her face when he said it, though his gaze dropped after. Ellie tried not to grimace. Breastfeeding and childbirth had taken a toll. But when Ty lifted his gaze to hers again, the heat in his eyes had gone from a slow burn to blazing.

"Jesus," he growled. "You're so fucking sexy."

A shuddery thrill raced through her, and Ellie leaned back a little on his lap. "Please touch me," she murmured. "Everywhere. *Hurry.*"

She didn't have to ask twice. Hell, she probably didn't need to ask at all, given the hunger in his eyes. His mouth found her nipple, and she gave a startled cry as he devoured her, sucking and nipping and making her squirm with pleasure.

"Ty," she gasped as he moved to the other side, devoting as much attention to that breast as he had to its twin. Ellie squirmed, feeling a bit like a teenager dry-humping on the living room sofa. She wriggled against him, surprised by the tingle of pleasure building inside her. *Jesus.* They weren't even naked.

"Don't stop," she gasped as she arched her hips to feel the rough scrape of denim against the softness of her core. Stars sparked behind her eyes, and Ellie cried out as Ty dragged his teeth over the underside of her breast.

"Oh, God," she moaned. "I think I'm going to—"

A blast of music burst from the speakers, making her freeze.

*"John Jacob Jingleheimer Schmidt! That's my name tooooo…!"*

Ellie blinked as a chorus of children's voices filled the room. Disoriented, she looked around, wondering if this was a bizarre dream and she was about to wake up with her nightie bunched around her hips and her eye mask tangled in her hair.

"Your iPod," Ty said, sliding his hand from her breast to the couch cushion. "I think you put your knee on it."

Sure enough, he extracted it from under her knee, holding it up, the display showing the cover of one of Henry's favorite kids' albums. Behind her, the music continued to blare.

*"Whenever I go out, the people always shout, there goes John, Jacob Jingleheimer Schmidt, nah-nah-nah-nah-nah-nah-nah…!"*

Ty clicked the stop button with his thumb and gave her an awkward smile. She stared at him a moment, then blew a lock of hair from her eye.

"Be honest with me," she said. "Is this the worst seduction attempt in the history of sex?"

Ty laughed and tossed the iPod aside. Before Ellie had a chance to be embarrassed, he reached for her again, sliding his hands to her ass to hold her against him. "You're perfect, Ellie."

A rush of affection bloomed in her chest, and Ellie fought the urge to tell him. To confess that she felt a whole lot more than simple lust.

*This is just sex.* She pushed those thoughts aside. *No falling for him.*

"Where were we?" he murmured, before planting a trail

of kisses between her breasts. "If I'm not mistaken, you were seconds from coming."

A flutter of excitement rippled through her, and Ellie nodded, amazed that he'd noticed. It's not like they were familiar enough with each other's bodies yet to pick up on cues. "It's been a while," Ellie murmured. "I might have a quick fuse right now."

"Good," Ty said, kissing her again. "Because if it's okay with you, I'd like to make you come at least a couple times tonight."

Ellie shuddered again, then groaned as Ty bent to suck her nipple into his mouth. She groaned and gripped the back of his head, so turned on she couldn't see straight.

"Ty," she gasped. "I want you. Please. I need more."

Grinning, he drew back and shifted her off his lap. Ellie curled her legs up under her as he shucked his jeans with impressive efficiency. He tossed them aside, then stood there gloriously naked and hard.

"I think we can make that happen," he said.

Several of the condoms had slipped into the space between the couch cushions, and Ellie made a mental note to find them all before Henry came home.

*Quit doing chores in your head.*

She growled and grabbed a condom, tearing it open before Ty had a chance to suggest they move to the bedroom.

There was something so sexy, so forbidden, so deliciously passionate about doing it right here on the sofa.

Also, she was pretty sure she couldn't wait the thirty seconds it would take to walk to the other end of the hall.

Reaching up, she slid the condom over him, relieved to see she'd managed to grab one with a more generous size—the condom, not his cock, though holy-mother-of-hell he was huge. She swallowed hard, wondering what it would feel like.

She doubted she'd have to wonder long.

"You're so fucking hot," he growled, dropping back on the couch and pulling her onto him.

His cock nestled against her, so close to her opening that just the tiniest shift would have him inside her. Arching her back, she ground against him.

Ty reached up and pushed her hair back from her face.

"You set the pace, El," he murmured.

But Ellie didn't want to go slow anymore. Angling up on her knees, she reached down and positioned his cock where she wanted it. Then she drew him inside, hesitating there with the tip of him clenched tight at her opening.

"Jesus," he hissed between his teeth.

Emboldened by his pleasure, Ellie sank down hard, crying out as he filled her completely. *So deep.*

*The man was huge.*

She took him in, crying out at the delicious friction against her core. The heat in his gaze, the spice in his aftershave, the salt of his skin—everything about this was giving her sensory overload. Pleasure flew at her from all angles, zapping her like lightning bolts, filling her ears and sizzling her skin.

Her hips seemed to be moving all on their own, taking what she craved, what she *needed*. She ground harder against him as the pleasure mounted. Ty threaded his fingers into her hair and pulled her down for a kiss.

"That's it, El," he whispered. "Use me."

She rocked against him as flickers of light danced behind her eyelids. It was ridiculous how fast this was happening, but she didn't object. She cried out as the first wave of orgasm hit her.

"Oh, God!" she screamed, thankful her brother didn't live next door anymore. Not that there was any way to contain it, so intense was the pleasure that blared through her body. "Ohmygod, Ty."

The intensity was unreal, pulsing through her whole core

as she ground against him. Her brain flashed on images of the Happy Jammer vibe, the one that claimed to hit the G-spot and clitoris at the same time.

*Happy Jammer has nothing on this man,* she thought as thick threads of pleasure spun through her, twirling and twisting and knotting up tight before releasing in a burst of color and friction.

When the sensation finally ebbed, she rocked her hips more slowly, then stopped altogether. She opened her eyes.

Ty grinned. "That was impressive."

Her lips tugged up. "I'm not usually that fast."

He laughed and stroked a palm over her breast, making her shudder. "I'll take that as a compliment."

"You should."

Still grinning, he dipped his head to kiss the underside of her breast. "Actually, I don't think I get much credit for that," he said. "That was all you, Ellie."

"It's, uh—been a while."

"You're very responsive," he said, curling his tongue around her nipple to make her shudder.

Ellie grinned and shifted on his lap. He was still rock hard and still deep inside her. As far as she could tell, he hadn't come yet.

"Want to slow things down a little for round two?" she murmured, rocking her hips just a little.

Ty laughed and moved his attention to her other breast. "You sure you don't need a second to rest?"

"No. I don't want to rest."

Heat flashed in his eyes, and he nodded once. "A woman who knows what she wants."

Before Ellie said anything, he slid an arm around her waist, gathering her against him. Then he lifted her up, sliding them both to the floor so he was on top of her.

She tilted her head back, marveling at the well-muscled

arms on either side of her head, at the weight of his body pinning her to the carpet. At the fact that he'd somehow stayed nestled inside her.

She arched up, signaling her readiness for more.

Ty laughed and eased back, then slid deep again. "You're amazing," he breathed, drawing back only to slide back in. "And you feel so good."

Ellie moaned and tilted her hips, amazed at how incredible he felt. The firmness of the floor, the hardness between her legs, everything about it was a delicious contrast to the soft heat inside her. She gasped as he drew back again then drove into her hard. She clawed at his back, spurring him on.

"Fuck, Ellie," he groaned. "You're driving me crazy."

His words rippled through her, morphing her into a sex goddess. That was new. Selling Madame Butterfly had empowered her, equipped her with a sexual knowledge she'd never had before. But putting it into practice, experiencing it with a man who triggered every last nerve in her body—that was something else entirely.

The sensation was building again, and Ellie wondered if he was close, too. His pace quickened, his breath was growing ragged. He slowed his movements, buying time. Hesitating.

She dug her heels into the back of his thighs. "Don't stop."

"El," he gasped. "If I don't slow down, I'm going to—"

"Do it!" she cried, amazed by her own boldness. "Please, Ty."

He hesitated only a second before complying, slamming into her again. His hips moved with shocking strength, driving in hard and deep. Ellie rose to meet him.

"That's it," she whispered. "Please. I'm close, too."

That's all it took to tip them both over the edge. He gave a low growl in the back of his throat and plunged in hard, hitting that spot again and again as he pulsed inside her.

"Ellie," he groaned, his weight pressing her shoulder

blades into the carpet. The rawness of that friction, the pulsing of heat inside her, the echo of his pleasure in her ears, ripped through her whole body, triggering one mind-blowing tremor after another until they both lay spent on her living room floor.

When they caught their breath, Ty rolled to one side and lay panting next to her. Ellie curled against him, warming as he slid an arm around her and pulled her to his chest.

"That was incredible," he said.

Ellie smiled to herself, giddy at what had just happened—thrilled by her own pleasure and that she'd managed to please him.

*Sex goddess indeed.*

She giggled, making Ty turn to look at her.

"Should I be offended that you're laughing after sex?"

Shaking her head, she leaned close and planted a kiss along his stubbled jaw. "Definitely not. I'm just happy."

"Me, too." He pulled her closer, burying his face in her hair. Ellie snuggled against him and rested the heel of her hand on his chest.

"I have a confession," she whispered. "That was my first casual hookup."

"Ever?"

"Yep." She smoothed her palm around his chest, making lazy circles over his heart. "I've never slept with anyone who wasn't a boyfriend or husband or something."

"Huh." There was a note of warmth in that single syllable, something that sounded almost like pride. "I'm honored."

Ellie giggled. "You should be."

"So, was it everything you expected?"

She nodded slowly, considering how she felt. Dreamy. Tingly. Mind-numbingly satisfied. "Yes," she said. "I loved it."

"Good." He pulled her closer, his face still buried in her hair as her fingers caressed his nipple. "Me, too."

She didn't say anything after that, content to stroke his chest as she savored the contours of his pecs, his abdomen, his ribs, then moved back over his heart. Her pulse still thudded in her ears as she circled her palm over the middle of his chest.

*You stay out of this*, she thought, not sure whether she was talking to his heart or hers.

# Chapter Nine

Ty woke with a start the next morning, mild alarm washing through him as he noticed he wasn't in his own bed.

The panic abated the moment he realized where he was.

"Morning," Ellie said, giving him a sleepy smile as she propped herself on one arm beside him. Her hair was rumpled, her cheek was pillow-creased, and she was the most beautiful woman he'd ever seen.

"Morning," Ty murmured, wanting her all over again.

"How'd you sleep?"

"Great," he said, surprised to realize it was true. He'd spent the whole night in her bed, which was rare for him. Sleepovers were not his thing. They made him edgy and restless.

Besides, spending the night at someone's house tended to spell "relationship" instead of "casual fling."

But as Ellie shifted under the covers and revealed a swath of skin at the top of one breast, Ty reconsidered his objections.

"Thanks for last night," Ellie said. "I had fun."

"Fun," Ty repeated cautiously, watching her face for signs that last night had meant more to her than that. Was she still okay with the casual-sex agreement they'd made?

Was he?

*Of course, you idiot,* he told himself, annoyed that his brain would even toy with the possibility of more. Not even with someone as amazing as Ellie.

"Last night was terrific," he said. "We should do it again sometime."

"For sure!"

Was he imagining things, or were they trying way too hard to sound breezy and casual? As Ellie sat up and slipped out of bed, Ty's imagination took a completely different turn. He admired her bare back, appreciating the curve of her breast as she moved through the doorframe and padded naked out the door. She returned seconds later, cinching the silky pink robe around her. His dick went hard under the covers, and he shifted the blankets around him so she wouldn't notice.

She wasn't meeting his eyes.

"So, Henry should be home around noon," Ellie said in a cheerfully casual tone that seemed forced. "I suppose we should get cleaned up and, uh…"

Ty sat up in bed. "I'll be out of here way before that."

Ellie sat down on the edge of the bed. "You don't have to run off. I was just letting you know so we wouldn't get carried away again."

She fidgeted with the sash on her robe, and he wondered what she was thinking. Did she have any regrets?

The sex had been amazing, no doubt. But so had everything that came after—dishing up fragrant helpings of salmon chowder to eat in bed, laughing together as they mopped the empty bowls with thick slabs of homemade sourdough. They'd snuggled and talked and then set the bowls aside to devour each other again.

It was a great night.

It was the best damn date of his life. Even without the sex, he would have thought so. Spending time with Ellie was like nothing he'd experienced before.

Ellie smiled, and the beauty of that simple gesture made his chest ache.

*Dumbass. Don't fall for her.*

Ty cleared his throat. "You doing okay?"

Ellie nodded and tossed her hair, still fiddling with the robe sash. "I'm great! You?"

"Never better. I just wanted to make sure you're still good with…well, *this*."

The words sounded lame once he'd said them out loud, but as relief lit her face, he knew they were exactly the right thing. She sat down on the edge of the bed, close, but not touching him. When she met his eyes, her sweetness took his breath away.

"I think so," she said slowly. "This is new to me, you know?"

"Sex without a relationship?"

"Exactly. I'm sitting here thinking I want to jump you again—"

"By all means," Ty offered. His dick throbbed.

Ellie laughed and kept going. "But I'm also thinking this is all sort of strange. Like I'm not sure how to act around you. Do we snuggle, or is that too relationshippy? Do we spend time together outside the bedroom, or is this just a sex thing? Or right now—do I get up and make you breakfast, or shoo you out of my house so I can tidy up before my family comes home?"

The raw honesty in her words filled him with warmth, and he took a moment to savor that before answering. "You definitely don't have to make me breakfast," he said. "That much I can answer. As for the rest of it, let's go with what feels right."

She gave him an uncertain look, and Ty scooted down on

the bed to place a hand on her knee. "You're nervous about Henry coming home, so you probably want a little space and downtime to get ready. Am I right?"

Ellie nodded, relieved. "Yes. Exactly."

"But you think it's rude to shove me out of the house before I have my pants on, and you're also not sure about the etiquette involved in hookups."

"Yes," she said, flashing him a grateful smile. "That's exactly right."

"Fuck the etiquette," he said. "It's our hookup. We make the rules."

"Yeah?"

"Yeah. I like spending time with you, Ellie. Not just the sex, but talking, eating—hell, fixing your sink."

"I like spending time with you, too." She smiled, and Ty's chest tightened. "I like the idea of hanging out with you sometimes. Outside the bedroom, I mean."

"That sounds great," he said. "We're on the same page, then."

"But I'm also used to having my own space," she said. "And it feels a little odd to wake up with a naked man in my house."

Ty grinned, touched by her honesty. "Ellie, you can ask for what you want. If you want space, ask for space. If you want to know what I'm thinking, ask what I'm thinking."

"I do want to know what you're thinking," she said, tucking a strand of hair behind one ear. "But I also kinda want to have you again. Just once more."

"Once," he repeated, trying not to let the dismay show on his face. "So, you're thinking of this as a one-time hookup?"

Ellie blinked then shook her head "No!" Her cheeks flushed a deeper shade of pink. "I meant once more this morning. Like—before my family comes home. After that— um—well. How about we just see?"

Ty laughed, still reeling from the surge of unexpected emotion. Still shocked to discover how much it stung in those five seconds he thought he might never get to have Ellie again.

He didn't like it one bit.

But he did like the way Ellie was looking at him now, with heat and desire and warmth flooding those bright blue eyes. Ty held out his hand and smiled. "Come here," he said, relieved when she put her hand in his without question. "Now that we've established the terms of our hookup, let's see how we do with the quickie."

Ellie laughed and let him pull her back down onto the bed, curving her body against his like she belonged there.

It took everything he had to convince his heart not to believe that.

. . .

Two hours later, Ty was home watching football and eating Doritos straight from the bag. They tasted stale and chalky, nothing at all like the homemade waffles and bacon Ellie had insisted on feeding him before he'd left her house just before eleven.

They'd said good-bye on her porch with a hug that warmed him to the core and a kiss that tasted faintly of maple syrup.

"Let's do this again sometime," Ty had murmured into her hair.

"Definitely."

Neither of them had named a date.

When his phone buzzed on the couch beside him, a jolt of excitement hit him in the gut. Maybe it was Ellie. Maybe she wanted to meet for lunch or set a date for later in the week.

He glanced at the readout on his phone and tried not to be disappointed at the sight of his sister's name.

"Hey, Anna," he said. "Sorry I haven't emailed back. Work's been crazy."

"No problem." Her voice was cheerful and much more understanding than he deserved. "Did you have a chance to figure out if any of those dates will work for you? To meet Martin, I mean."

"Right, yes." He tried to remember the dates she'd listed, pretty sure the next week was wide open. "I was thinking next Friday."

"Ugh. I was afraid you'd pick that one."

"Am I too late?"

"No, it's not your fault. It's just that my new in-laws called last night and asked to take us out that night to celebrate. They're super jazzed about the wedding. Martin is an only child, so they're going crazy putting engagement announcements in the paper and offering to help with wedding plans."

"Is that a good thing or a bad thing?"

"Good, I think. Actually, really great. I've had friends complain about their meddling in-laws, but I don't feel like that," she said. "Honestly, it's just nice to have someone care. My mom isn't into weddings, and, obviously, Dad's not involved."

"Obviously," Ty muttered, the familiar prickle of ice trickling through his chest.

"I guess it's kinda fun to have family that takes an interest."

"Shit, I'm sorry." Ty closed his eyes, wishing he'd done a better job of being there for his sister. He hated the thought of disappointing her. "I know I haven't always been there for you, and I promise—"

"What? No, Ty—that's not what I meant at all," she said. "You're a great brother. I was talking about adults."

He snorted and stuck a hand in the Doritos bag. "And all this time I thought I did a pretty good job impersonating a grown-up."

Anna laughed. "You know what I mean. Parental figures. My mom had so many different boyfriends after Dad left, and they were all such jerks. Between that and Dad making all kinds of promises he'd end up breaking because he was going back to prison, I kinda learned a bad father figure is worse than none at all, you know?"

Ty did know. He found himself nodding, which was dumb. It wasn't like Anna could see him. But whether she meant to or not, her words struck chords deep inside him.

"Yeah," he said. "I think we both learned the only things you could count on grown-ups for was disappointment."

"Sometimes, that's true," she murmured. "Anyway, that's what I meant. Just that it's nice having Martin's parents fussing over me now. It's like I finally have the parents I always wished for. I'm pretty attached to them."

*Attached.* Something about that word made him think of Ellie, reminded him of his resolve not to fall for her. It was asking for disappointment. For her, for him, for her son—for all of them.

Ty's chest hurt, and his fingers traced his tattoo through his shirt. Fucking Johnny Cash, his father's idol. A constant reminder of where he'd come from.

He took a few breaths to get his voice under control. "I'm happy for you, Anna. Seriously."

"Thanks. I can totally reschedule Friday if that's the only day that'll work for you."

"Nah, that's fine. How about Thursday?"

"Thursday works! Or Monday, or Tuesday, or Wednesday—" She laughed, and Ty found himself smiling again. "Pretty much any day next week is good for me."

"I'm open, too," he said. "Pick one of those days and let me know."

"Will do!" She laughed again. "I'm so excited for you to

meet Martin!" She sounded delighted, and Ty flashed back to a memory of his happy, pigtailed kid sister when they were little. It was one of the only times they'd lived in the same household. He remembered someone shouting in the apartment next door, and the smell of Twinkies, and the warmth of his sister's shoulder pressed against his as they waited at the door for their father to come home from a meeting with his parole officer.

They'd waited all night. Waited until the social worker came and took them away.

He was jarred from the past by the dull beep of another call coming in. Pulling the phone from his ear, he glanced at the screen and his heart sped up.

*Ellie Sanders.*

"Ty? Do you want to get that?"

"Yeah," he said. "I kinda do."

"Oooh," Anna said, sounding giddy. "You totally got all melty-chocolate-voiced just then."

"Melty-chocolate-voiced? What the—"

"Answer it!" she ordered. "Don't keep your girlfriend waiting. Love you!"

"Love you, too. Lunatic."

She laughed and clicked off, leaving Ty to answer Ellie's call with his heart thumping solidly in his chest. "Hey, Ellie." He did his best to sound casual, playing it cool so she wouldn't guess how happy he was she'd called.

"Hey there," she said, equally breezy. Good. They could do this. Just two consenting adults having a casual relationship with no feelings involved.

"So, you can totally say no to this," she said. "There's no pressure at all. I swear it's not a big deal, and I almost hate to ask you at all. In fact, maybe I—"

"Ellie."

"Yeah?"

"Just spit it out." He didn't realize he was smiling until he caught sight of his own reflection in the mirror beside his front door. He looked away, reluctant to admit how much he loved the sound of her voice.

"Okay," she said. "But let me start again. How's your day going?"

He laughed and shoved the Doritos bag off his lap, nudging it onto the coffee table. "It's going great," he said. "Watching some football. I was just on the phone with my sister."

"You have a sister?" She sounded surprised.

"Yeah," he said, surprised at himself for mentioning it. He rarely talked about his family. Not with co-workers or women he dated—or anyone, really. "We have the same father, but different mothers."

"Oh. Are you close with your mom?"

"My mom died when I was two," he said.

He clenched his jaw, remembering the distaste in Anna's mother's eyes. "I'm not raising him," she'd growled at the social worker who'd come to check on them after Ty's dad had been hauled off to prison again. "He looks just like that son-of-a-bitch who spawned him."

"I'm so sorry," Ellie said, shaking Ty back to the conversation. She sounded more heartbroken than he would have expected, and he wondered why he was telling her any of this. It wasn't like him to volunteer so much personal information, and he kicked himself for putting a damper on their conversation. He tried to think of something more cheerful to say, but Ellie beat him to it.

"Your sister—what's her name?"

"Anna," he said. "She's getting married in a couple months."

"That's wonderful," Ellie said. "Are you in the wedding?"

"I'm walking her down the aisle." He heard the pride in

his own voice and wondered if Ellie heard it, too. "She asked me last week."

"That's so sweet," she said. "I'd always thought I'd have my brother do that when I got married. Our parents died when I was still pretty young, so he basically raised me."

"So, Jason walked you down the aisle when you married Henry's dad?"

"No, we ended up eloping." There was a hint of sadness in Ellie's voice, though he heard her trying to hide it. "Chuck wasn't big on weddings, so we ended up going to Vegas."

Ty scrubbed a hand over his chin and made a mental note to do whatever it took to ensure his sister had more pleasant wedding memories than Ellie did. "Your brother seems like a good guy," Ty said. "He always goes out of his way to chat up the staff when he visits Miriam."

"Yeah, he's the best," Ellie said. "He's been like a father to Henry."

Something knotted sharp and hard in his chest, but couldn't think of anything to say to that.

He cleared his throat. "What did you call to ask me?"

"What? Oh, right—sorry, I almost forgot." He heard her take a deep breath and braced himself for the question. "Henry's school has this musical production coming up on Thursday night. They had a parent all lined up to film it, but the guy has to travel for work at the last minute. They're trying to find someone else to fill in with a video camera, and I was wondering if maybe you'd be willing to—"

"You said Thursday?"

"Yes. This Thursday."

Ty hesitated, hearing his sister's voice in his head.

*"Thursday works! Or Monday, or Tuesday, or Wednesday—pretty much any day next week is good for me."*

But he didn't want to be like his dad, always changing things at the last minute. Even though he wanted to help Ellie out, he had to put his sister first.

He cleared his throat. "Sorry," he said. "I have dinner plans with my sister that night. I'm meeting her fiancé for the first time."

"Oh! That's great. And no problem. It's not a big deal."

"Some other time, maybe," Ty said, feeling like a Grade A jerk. His sister's words were still echoing in his head, but now they weren't the ones about the date. They were the other words.

*"My mom had so many different boyfriends after Dad left, and they were all such jerks. Between that and Dad making all kinds of promises he'd end up breaking because he was going back to prison, I kinda learned a bad father figure is worse than none at all, you know?"*

"Sorry," he said to Ellie, wishing there were some way to make it up to her.

*It's better this way,* he told himself. *Easier to draw lines, to set boundaries. To make sure no one gets hurt.*

"It's no problem at all," she said. "I'm sure we'll find someone else. Don't worry about it."

She sounded sincere, but Ty felt like a dick anyway. His chest was tight, and he wanted to pull her against it and feel the knot of tension release. He wanted to run his hand down her back, stroking her hair, kissing the crown of her head the way he'd done last night.

But none of that was in the cards for him.

"Some other time," Ty murmured, knowing there'd never be a time he'd be the kind of guy Ellie deserved.

• • •

Ellie did her best to tread carefully with Ty as they worked together in the studio over the next week. She was the ultimate professional while recording voiceovers and shooting footage for her new web videos, making sure not to do anything to suggest she wanted more than the fling they'd agreed to.

She *didn't,* obviously, so that part was easy. Mostly, anyway.

Okay, so once or twice she caught herself wondering what it would be like to have something with Ty that went beyond a casual hookup. What it would be like to go out on dates together, or to spend time just the three of them, her and Henry and Ty.

But that's not what she wanted. *Please.* After the way things ended with Chuck, there was no way she wanted to start down that path again. Not even with a guy like Ty.

*Ty.*

Her heart somersaulted, but she fought off the feeling. He didn't want a relationship any more than she did. It was better this way, especially with life as busy as it had been lately. Her Madame Butterfly parties were booked solid for the next three months, and things were crazy-busy with Henry's school stuff and the studio work with Ty. They were easy and friendly with each other, and not awkward at all, which was a relief.

"What are you up to tonight?"

Ty's question at the end of their recording session on Friday caught her by surprise, and it took her a second to formulate a response.

"Henry and I are making homemade corndogs for dinner," she said. "Maybe going for a walk to the park."

She waited, wondering why he'd asked. Was he wanting another hookup, or just being polite? Part of her hoped for the former. Henry had been begging for a sleepover at Jason and Miriam's, excited about practicing the new tent pitching skills Uncle Jason had taught him on their campout.

"I have tickets to see the Hillsboro Hops baseball game," Ty said. "Thought maybe you guys would like to go."

*You guys.* Ellie studied him. "You mean Henry and me?"

"Yeah. I asked Miriam and Jason, too, plus a couple other

folks on staff. I just did a big video project for the team, and the manager gave me a dozen tickets for tonight's game."

Was it like a date, or more of a professional engagement? Either way, the guy was offering to take her whole damn family to a ball game. She'd be an idiot to question it too much.

"I'd love to," she said. "What time should we meet you there?"

"I can come get you," he said. "That way we can head out there at the same time as Miriam and Jason."

"Henry will be thrilled. When should we be ready?"

"How about six? We can grab corndogs at the game."

"That sounds nice."

And it did sound nice, even if she wasn't entirely sure what she'd agreed to.

Miriam was no help when Ellie jogged down the street to their place that evening to borrow a baseball cap.

"We have several hundred employees between First Impressions and Speak Up," Miriam pointed out as she threaded Ellie's ponytail through the back of the Hillsboro Hops ball cap. "He could have invited any of them, but he didn't."

"Well, he invited you, too," Ellie pointed out.

"It's a ruse," Miriam insisted. "Know what else is a ruse?"

"What?"

Miriam grinned. "The fact that Jason invited Henry over after the game to set up the tent in our backyard and practice their camping skills. It's all a sneaky scheme to give you a night alone with lover boy."

"Miriam." Ellie rolled her eyes, not sure whether to thank her or smack her.

"Hey, I remember what it's like in the early stages of a relationship when you can't think about anything but shagging each other silly," she said. "I wanted to help out."

"It's *not* a relationship," Ellie insisted, even as a funny little ripple of joy shuddered through her.

When Ty arrived wearing a Hillsboro Hops shirt and a sexy five-o'clock shadow, the ripple became a flood. He grinned at her as he climbed the steps to join her on the porch.

"Cute," he said, tapping the bill of her ball cap before looking down at Henry. "Hey, little man! I like yours, too."

"Thank you." Henry adjusted his cap and smiled up at Ty. "My uncle Jason gave it to me. We're camping tonight."

"Is that so?" He looked at Ellie. His expression didn't change, but she thought she caught a spark in his eye. It was enough to make her insides do a melty little quiver.

*Lust,* she told herself. *It's only lust. That's all.*

"They're camping just down the street in their backyard," Ellie said, wanting to rein in her own expectations as well as his. "Only a block away."

"Good to know," Ty said. "You guys ready to head out?"

Ellie nodded and reached behind her to grab her purse off the entry table.

"I hope it's okay, but I told Miriam and Jason we'd carpool with them."

"I'm not sure we'll all fit." Ty nodded toward his pickup parked at the curb. "My truck's pretty tight for five."

"Jason offered to drive," she said. "They just got that new SUV, and there's already a booster seat in back for Henry."

Ty frowned. "I didn't even think about the booster seat."

Something dark passed through his eyes, and Ellie laid a hand on his arm.

"It's okay," she assured him. "I know you're not used to the whole kid thing."

"Right," he said, clearing his throat. "Yeah, that's great. It's way safer for Henry for us all to go with them."

There was a funny note in his voice, but he offered her a smile that looked real, albeit a little weak. Before she had a chance to ask about it, Jason stepped out onto the porch next door with a toolbox in one hand. He set it down, wiping his hands on a rag before offering one to Ty.

"Hey, man," Jason said, clasping Ty's hand. "Good to see you again."

"You, too."

"Thanks for fixing Ellie's plumbing the other night," he said. "Helluva patch job you did there."

Ty grimaced and glanced at Ellie. "I—uh—did my best with the tools on hand."

"No, it's great!" Jason said. "You were spot-on about the water heater corroding the pipes. That thing must've been thirty years old. I've got a new one ordered, so hopefully she'll be set for a while."

"She's lucky to have you."

Was it Ellie's imagination, or did Ty's voice sound funny? She couldn't place the emotion, but her heart did a soft little squeeze as she watched Henry reach up and tug the edge of Ty's sleeve.

"I've been practicing my lion face," he said. "Wanna see?"

"Definitely," Ty said.

"Rawr!" Henry raised his hands like claws, pawing at the air with impressive exuberance. Ellie laughed and tapped the brim of her son's cap, pleased when Ty high-fived him.

"Nice work." Ty looked at Ellie, grinning. "You want to show me your lion face?"

"Maybe later," she said, shooting him a conspiratorial grin. "Everyone ready to roll?"

"I'm ready!" Miriam shouted as she came hurrying up the walk with her belly round under a maternity baseball jersey. "Sorry, I had to pee again."

"Thanks for sharing." Jason picked up the toolbox again and rested the other hand in the small of his wife's back. He gave her a fond smile as he guided her toward the car and got her settled before shoving the toolbox in the hatchback.

Ellie turned to follow, unconsciously reaching down to grab Henry's hand. But he was two steps behind her and still looking up at Ty.

"Can I sit next to him?" Henry asked her, pointing a chubby finger up at Ty.

Ellie held her breath, hoping this wasn't weird for him. He didn't look alarmed, but it was tough to know what he was thinking.

"How come, baby?" she asked Henry.

"He's my friend and we work together now," Henry reported.

Ty, bless his heart, didn't miss a beat. "That's right," he said, resting a hand on Henry's shoulder. "You did a great job helping out at the studio. And it's great you've been practicing the lion face."

"Thanks!" Henry called, reaching up to grab Ty's hand as they started toward the car. "Do you have my paycheck?"

Ty froze. "Paycheck?"

"Yeah. When we were at your office, you said maybe I could be on the payroll and help with taxes and stuff."

"Oh." Ty frowned and shot Ellie a desperate look. "I, uh…"

"That was just a joke, sweetie," Ellie said, stepping in to rescue Ty. She steered her son to the car and opened the back door for him. Henry scrambled in, seemingly unfazed. "But we can definitely find some chores for you to do around the house to start earning more of an allowance."

Henry grinned and shoved his glasses up his nose. "Cool."

Ellie glanced back to see Ty still frozen in place, horror on his face.

"Ty?"

He started walking again, then bent down to peer into the car. "I'm so sorry about that, little man. I shouldn't have made that joke."

"That's okay," Henry said, offering a gap-toothed smile.

"No, really." Ty scrubbed a hand over his chin, clearly upset. "I didn't mean to let you down."

Ellie gave him a reassuring smile as she slid into the car next to Henry. She buckled her seat belt, then looked up to see Ty still standing on the sidewalk, a remorseful expression on his face. "Ty? You coming?"

"Yeah," he said, not moving. "Of course."

She patted the seat beside her, not sure what had him so upset. "Are you okay?"

He nodded, but the frown stayed fixed on his face. "Yeah," he said, ducking down to slide into the backseat beside her. "Never better."

Ellie studied the side of his face, noticing the grim set of his jaw. She committed it to memory, wanting to remember exactly what he looked like when he wasn't telling the whole truth.

# Chapter Ten

Ty spent the whole game kicking himself for his missteps with Ellie and Henry. What kind of idiot didn't even consider that a kid would need a car seat?

Not only that, but he'd disappointed Henry. The misunderstanding with the paycheck was a kick in the gut to Ty, so he could only imagine what it felt like to Henry.

*You don't have to imagine,* his subconscious reminded him. *You know exactly what it's like to have a grown-up let you down. And now you're doing the same damn thing, just like your old man.*

To Henry's credit, he seemed totally fine. Besides that, Ellie assured him at least half a dozen times it was no big deal.

"It's important for his development that he learn there's a difference between jokes and things to take literally," she said as she swirled her corndog in a puddle of mustard while Henry chased after a fly ball with his uncle. "It's part of growing up."

She sounded so certain that he almost believed it. But he couldn't forget that flash of disappointment he'd seen in Henry's eyes. "I feel like I let him down," Ty said. "He should be able to trust grown-ups not to disappoint him."

Ellie rested a hand on his knee. "He's a tough kid who survived leukemia," she'd pointed out. "Small things like that don't even register on his radar."

Her reassurance made it worse. He'd disappointed a kid who'd had cancer, for crying out loud. What kind of asshole did something like that?

*The kind of asshole who teaches his three-year-old to open a beer.*

But Ty did his best not to dwell on it.

And he had a great time at the game, sitting shoulder-to-shoulder with Ellie, making corndog runs for Miriam, sipping beer with Jason, and scrambling with Henry to catch a pop fly at the bottom of the seventh inning.

Henry was still clutching the ball as he slept in the backseat on the way home. Ty glanced at the boy with his freckle-dusted nose and little glasses askew on his face, and for the first time in his life, he wondered what it would feel like to be a dad.

"Here we are!" Miriam announced from the front seat. "Rise and shine, little buddy. Time to do some camping."

Henry roused, confused for a moment until his gaze landed on Ty. "Hey," he said. "Thank you for the fun time."

"You're very welcome," Ty said. "I liked hanging out with you."

It was totally true, and that surprised the crap out of him.

Ellie doled out hugs and reminded Henry to be on his best behavior with his aunt and uncle. The boy assured her he would.

"I make extra sure I put up the seat when I pee and put down the seat so other people can poop," Henry announced.

"Good man," Ty told him. "You're well on your way to becoming a well-mannered gentleman."

"A well-mannered gentleman who still needs to learn

when it's appropriate to talk about poop and pee," Ellie said with a sternness Ty recognized as a cover for amusement.

"Maybe he'll become a urologist," Jason pointed out. "Or a proctologist. Then he can talk about poop and pee all he wants."

"I'm going to be Batman when I grow up," Henry insisted.

"Or that," Ty said. "It's good to have career goals."

Ellie kissed her son once more, then stepped back with her hand on the door. "You'll call if you need anything?" she asked her brother.

"Relax, El," Jason said. "We're pitching a tent in the yard, not backpacking into the Three Sisters Wilderness to go snow camping."

"Don't think he hasn't suggested the latter," Miriam muttered. "I'll make sure they're properly roped-up if they decide to practice climbing techniques on the roof."

"That's reassuring," Ellie said as she closed the car door then waved as they drove away. She turned and gave Ty a sheepish smile. "On a scale of one to ten, how neurotic is it that I fret about him when he's sleeping a block away from home?"

"I think it's in my best interest not to answer," he said, reaching up to tuck a stray strand of hair back under her baseball cap. A warm, clover-scented breeze tugged it loose again, making him smile. "I also think it's sweet," he added. "The way you are with Henry. The way you are with your brother and Miriam."

She grinned, her blue eyes shimmering the way they always seemed to when she talked about family. "They're the best. They'll be great parents."

"Seems like they've had a lot of practice with Henry."

Ty had watched in awe all evening, amazed by how everyone seemed to magically know the right way to handle the kid.

Everyone but him, that is.

"Anyway, thanks so much for inviting us." Ellie touched his arm, sending a current of energy along the surface of his flesh. "Everyone had a great time."

Ty nodded, shifting his keys from one hand to the other. The air was still warm, though the sun was already halfway gone. Crickets had started to chirp, and he wondered whether he should kiss her or not. He urgently wanted to, but what was the etiquette here? How did a friends-with-benefits arrangement work with a single mom? He didn't want to presume anything.

He was still debating when Ellie solved the problem for him. "Would you like to come in for a drink?"

He'd never wanted anything more, but he held back a little. What was it about Ellie that left him so undone? That made him question whether he could pull off a no-strings-attached arrangement? Nothing like that had never happened before, not once in his entire life.

*She's inviting you in for a glass of water, not a marriage proposal,* he reminded himself. *Get a grip, Hendrix.*

Still, he hesitated. "Are you sure?" he asked.

"Positive." She grinned, and Ty's pulse kicked up. "Come on."

She led the way into her house, and Ty followed her into the kitchen. She pulled open the fridge and frowned. "Okay, here's where I confess that inviting you in for a drink was just a ruse," she said. "All I have is milk, grape juice, and water."

He smiled and stepped up beside her, closing the distance between them. "It's fine, El. I didn't come in for your grape juice."

Ellie smiled and turned to face him, mischief sparking in her blue eyes. "What did you come in for?"

He didn't answer. Not with words, anyway. Cupping her face in one hand, he drew her mouth to his and kissed her hard and deep. She melted a little against him, her whole body soft and familiar. As he stroked her bare arm, he wondered if the same zaps of emotion were pulsing through her body. Was he the only idiot whose heart kept trying to dive headfirst into the swimming pool with no lifeguard after they'd already declared the water off-limits?

He broke the kiss and looked into her eyes, struggling to keep himself under control. "I've been wanting to do that all evening," he said.

Ellie slid her palms up his chest, thrilling him with the warmth of her touch. "Me, too." She grinned wider. "Want to know what else I've been wanting to do all night?"

Ty's pulse started to gallop. His mouth was too dry to form words, so he just nodded. "Yeah."

"Come on." She grabbed his hand and towed him down the hall toward the bedroom. Closing the door behind them, she flipped the lock and gave him a sheepish look. "Just in case."

He smiled, grateful for the knowledge that the duplex next door was vacant and that he and Ellie had the house to themselves for the whole night.

Ty stepped forward and reached for her again, drawing her against him with deliberate gentleness. "Can we go slow this time?"

She nodded, eyes flashing in the light from her bedside lamp. "That sounds heavenly."

*Heaven.* That's exactly what this was like, holding her in his arms again. "I want this to last," he murmured.

There was something deeper in those words, in the emotion behind them. He started to explain, but the warmth her eyes told him he didn't need to. Was she feeling this, too?

She tilted her head back, and Ty kissed her deeply, taking his time, memorizing the sweetness of her mouth, the curve of her cheek under his palm, the softness of her breasts pressed against his chest. He moved them both toward the bed, not breaking the kiss as he walked her backward until she bumped the edge of the mattress. She was still wearing her baseball cap, and he pulled it off and tossed it aside.

"May I?" he asked as the started to tug the elastic from her ponytail.

She nodded and smiled up at him. "I love when you do that," she murmured. "Put your hands in my hair."

Ty loved it, too. The soft threads slid through his fingers like liquid silk, and he breathed in the orangey scent of her shampoo. He kissed her again, deeper this time, then drew back to meet her eyes.

"Lie back," he murmured.

Ellie didn't argue. Just boosted herself onto the edge of the bed with a smile. She hesitated there, angling up to kiss him again. Ty eased her back, using the weight of his body to press her down against the coverlet. She went willingly, bare legs curved over the edge of the bed as she smiled up at him.

"Take off your shirt," she whispered. "I want to look at you."

He sat up and grabbed the hem of his T-shirt. Self-consciousness flickered through him as her gaze moved over his tattoo. But she didn't linger there. She took in the whole of him—chest, abs, shoulders—then came back up to his face. When she smiled, something stirred in the center of his chest.

"You are a very well-made specimen, Mr. Henrdix," she said.

He laughed. It would have sounded dorky coming from anyone else, but those words from Ellie were fucking adorable. And hot. But also adorable.

"I want to taste you, Ellie."

Her response was a low moan that made his lips pulse as he kissed his way along her throat and down, over her sternum, her belly—

"Ty." She clutched his shoulders as he slid lower, unbuttoning her thin cotton sundress as he kissed a trail down the middle of her body. By the time he reached the edge of her panties, she was breathless and squirming, with Ty kneeling on the floor in front of her.

Ellie reached down and raked her fingers through his hair, urging him on.

"Please," she gasped.

The need was in her eyes as much as her words. He got the message loud and clear. Nudging her legs apart, he kissed one hipbone then the other, pausing to plant a line of kisses down one bare thigh. Her panties were pink and lacy, and part of him wanted to just rip them off.

But he took his time, brushing his lips over the soft slope of one bare knee before working his way to the other, then back up. He scooped his hands under her, cupping her gently with his palms. Ellie moaned as his chin grazed the lace-covered heat at her center.

"Ty," she gasped. "I want you so much."

"I can tell."

God, that sounded cocky, but it was true. She was damp with need, the same need that throbbed through him. But he wanted to pleasure her first.

Hooking his thumbs under the edge of her panties, he hesitated a moment. Ellie lifted her hips, and Ty dragged the lace down her thighs, baring her completely.

"Beautiful," he murmured. "So goddamn beautiful."

A muffled laugh was her response, but her fingers in his hair were a sort of plea. He leaned closer, letting his breath graze her. Then his tongue, softly at first as he probed her center. The instant he touched her clit, she cried out. Her hips rose off the bed, an invitation for Ty to bury his face completely. He was gentle to start, then more exuberant as he began to devour her. She tasted so fucking good, and he gripped her hips to hold her steady as she bucked against him.

"Oh, God!" she cried. "Don't stop."

He wouldn't dream of it. And he couldn't get enough of her, sucking and licking savoring her softness against his mouth.

"God, Ellie," he groaned against her. "You taste so good."

She laughed, then gasped as he stroked the length of her with his tongue. "Ty," she gasped. "I've never felt anything like—"

A pleasured gasp took the place of words, and Ty wondered what she'd been about to say. But he knew. Somehow, he knew because the same damn words were vibrating through his brain.

*I've never felt anything like this.*

But it wasn't just the pleasure.

He grazed her with the tip of his tongue again, and she tensed in his palms. She was getting close. He could tell. Her breath quickened, and she arched up tight against his mouth. "Ty," she gasped. "I'm so close."

"Let go, baby."

She gave a low moan and fisted her hands in the duvet, her whole body arching up to meet him. He slid one finger inside her, rewarded by the tight clench of her around him. She grabbed the pillow next to her head and pulled it to her face, smothering her cries of pleasure.

He didn't stop until she went still, until he was sure she'd wrung every last drop of pleasure from the orgasm. At last, Ty slid to one side and planted a kiss on her hipbone. Ellie pushed the pillow off her face, then sat up on her elbows and looked at him.

"Holy shit," she said. "That was like something out of a book."

He laughed and rubbed his chin against his bare shoulder. He still tasted her and wondered if there was some way to keep that with him forever. "I don't know what kind of books you read, but I need to download some."

She laughed and shook her head, her wide blue eyes and disheveled hair making her look a little wild. "You have no idea how good that felt."

Ty grinned. "I might have some idea."

She smiled as Ty stood up and eased onto the bed, curling his body around her. He was still wearing his jeans, but her skin was smooth against his bare chest. He held her like that until her breathing slowed. Until her heartbeat returned to normal beneath his palm. He would have held her forever, honestly, if her stomach hadn't growled.

"God, that's embarrassing." She giggled and skimmed a hand over her bare belly. "Sorry. I gave half my corndog to Henry after he dropped his, so I guess I'm still hungry."

"You didn't get another one?"

She shook her head, blond hair fanning out on the bedspread behind her. "I was too busy cheering for the game."

"Wait here."

He didn't give her a chance to protest. Just jumped off the bed and headed for the kitchen, grateful he was already familiar with the space. Her skillets hung on a rack above the stove, and he stuck one on the burner and cranked the heat before turning to pillage her fridge.

Ten minutes later, he carried the plate into the bedroom. Ellie was sitting up, the silky pink robe tucked around her, and she peered at him with curiosity. "What on earth—"

"I hope you don't mind, but I saw eggs and parmesan when you had the fridge open earlier." He dragged a heavy bolster pillow to the center of the bed and set the plate on it, then handed her a fork. "My grandmother used to make this for me."

"What is it?" She took a bite before he responded, then closed her eyes in the same blissed-out expression she'd worn just twenty minutes ago. Ty tried not to feel jealous of eggs.

"Oh my God, this is amazing."

He grinned. "It's super simple. My grandma had this big cast iron skillet. She'd throw down a layer of the cheese, and then just as it started getting crispy, she'd break an egg on it and let that cook."

"This is like crack on a plate." She took another bite and sighed with pleasure. "I wish I'd known about this when I was pregnant with Henry. All I wanted was eggs and cheese, but I never had anything like this."

Those words should have freaked him out. So should the fact that he was sharing intimate memories of his grandmother. But none of that seemed strange. His pulse was thrumming along like normal, and it was the most natural thing in the world to sit here half-naked on Ellie's bed watching her eat a plate of eggs he'd made for her.

A lock of hair fell across her forehead, and Ty reached up to tuck it behind her ear.

*God, she's beautiful.*

He didn't say the words out loud, but she smiled at him as though he had. The loveliness of her expression made his heart split wide open.

When she finished eating, she set the plate aside and grinned at him. "Thank you so much, Ty. For the snack, for—um, for everything else." Her cheeks pinkened a little, and she gave him a shy smile. "I loved that."

The words snagged on a corner of his brain, confusing him for a second. It wasn't for a few more breaths that he realized what she'd said.

I loved *that*.

At first, he'd thought she'd said *you*.

And for the briefest moment, he didn't hate the idea.

# Chapter Eleven

Monday morning, Ty was putting the finishing touches on a new video when his Spidey senses tingled. He was wearing headphones, so it wasn't footsteps that alerted him to Ellie's presence.

It was something about Ellie. Like he'd *felt* her somehow, which was dumb.

"Ellie," he said, annoyed by the happy note in his voice. "Thanks for coming."

She smiled and strode into the office, flushed and lovely in a pair of bike shorts with a helmet tucked under one arm. "Sorry I'm late." She moved around the edge of his desk to sit down in the chair he'd pulled up close beside him. "Mondays are the only time I can sneak in a bike ride before I pick Henry up at school."

"Not a problem. I think it's great you're able to find time for stuff like that."

She looked at him a little oddly, and Ty wanted to grimace at the absurdity of his words. It was just that Ellie didn't fit the mold of what he'd always thought a single mom would be.

Sure, she was doting and kind and the best mother he'd ever seen in action.

But she was also independent and smart and so damn sexy he couldn't stop thinking about her.

*Knock it off, Hendrix. You're ogling a woman with helmet-hair and a sweaty T-shirt.*

"You're so beautiful," he blurted.

Ellie laughed and rolled her eyes. "You've now seen me in a soggy dress and sweaty workout gear. The fact that you can say that with a straight face means you're either nuts or the world's best liar."

Ty grinned, not bothering to correct her. She had to know how stunning she was, right?

"So." Ellie propped her bike helmet on the desk and smiled at him. "You wanted to see me about the kombucha videos?" Her smile wavered a little. "Wait, don't tell me they hated them."

"On the contrary." He turned and grabbed a basket off the far edge of his desk and pulled it toward him. He plucked out two fancy wineglasses and a brown bottle filled with murky liquid. "Everyone at Mama Jama's Kombucha totally loved the video. They especially loved your voiceover work. Said you were the perfect sound for the brand."

"Oh." She smiled and swiped a strand of damp hair off one cheek. "That's wonderful."

"They sent us this gift basket as a thank you," he said. "It's a bunch of new flavors they're testing out. I thought you might like to make a date of it."

Ellie grinned and grabbed the neckline of her shirt, fluttering it back and forth to get some air. "If I'd known this was a date, I would have washed the mud off my legs first."

Ty glanced down at her legs and shook his head. "You're perfect."

He meant it, too. He loved that she wasn't afraid to get

dirty, in all senses of the word. Figuring he should stop gaping at her legs, he turned and popped the top on the first bottle, then poured some into each long-stemmed glass.

Handing one to Ellie, he pulled the second glass toward him. Then he tore open the accompanying package of crackers, frowning at the label that touted them as gluten-free, soy-free, nut-free, and dairy-free.

"Holy spunk-trumpet," he muttered. "What's even in these things?"

Ellie snorted into her wineglass, fanning herself as she set it down on his desk. "You're the most creative curser of anyone I've ever met," she said. "I can't believe you learned that from your grandmother."

"She was British," he said. "I think that's where some of it came from."

Ty shoved a cardboard-tasting cracker in his mouth and chewed, fighting back the wave of nostalgia that made his stomach churn. Or maybe that was the cracker. He took a sip of kombucha to wash it down, then made a face.

"God, that's awful," he said, wiping his mouth with the back of his hand.

"I wasn't going to say anything." Ellie set down her own glass and grimaced. "But now that you mention it, the flavor profile is…um…interesting."

"That's one way to put it."

"It tastes like Rice-a-Roni mixed with raspberry jam and bubblegum."

Ty laughed as he turned the bottle around and peered at the label. "Apparently they were going for Sageberry Sunrise, whatever the hell that is."

"Huh." Ellie took another sip and grimaced. "Maybe it's an acquired taste."

"Let's try another flavor." Ty emptied both glasses into an empty Big Gulp cup on the edge of his desk, then pried the top off another bottle. He poured smaller servings this time, having learned his lesson.

*That's the only lesson you seem to have learned,* his subconscious chided. *You weren't supposed to get attached here, remember?*

Ty shook his head and focused on pouring the kombucha. He wasn't falling for Ellie. Just sleeping with her, that's all.

"Gah!" he muttered as the bubbly beverage foamed over the edge of the glass, spilling onto a stack of papers. "Filthy wank stain."

"Exactly," Ellie said as she grabbed a wad of tissues from the box on his desk and sponged up the mess. Ty relocated the paperwork to the opposite corner, while Ellie sat back down and picked up her glass.

"So your grandma had British roots and the world's most creative swearword vocabulary," she said. "What else did you get from her?"

Ty mopped the corner of his laptop with a Kleenex, only half focused on his answer. "The knowledge that everyone either leaves you or dies, so there's no sense getting attached to anyone, ever."

*Holy shit.* Did he just say that out loud?

He glanced up to see Ellie looking as stunned as he felt. Embarrassed, Ty picked up his glass and took a big gulp. He tried to laugh, hoping to convince her he'd been joking, but all he managed to do was inhale an extra-big helping of foul-tasting kombucha.

"Wow." Ellie took a dainty sip of her own drink. "I was thinking more like eye color or the ability to touch your nose with your tongue. That's — I'm sorry, Ty. It sounds like you had it rough."

"It wasn't that bad." He cleared his throat, wanting to convince himself as much as he wanted to convince her. "I'm fine now."

He shook his head and set his glass down, feeling like the biggest dumbass on the planet. Why had he said that? He didn't share personal details with anyone. *Anyone.* Why was he blurting out his deepest secrets to Ellie?

*Because you like her. A lot more than you meant to.*

The thought left a funny taste in his mouth. Or maybe that was the kombucha.

"Ugh." He took another tentative sip, but the flavor hadn't improved. "This one tastes like feet."

"No, not feet." Ellie took another dainty sip, seemingly unfazed by Ty's inability to have a normal human conversation. How did she do that?

She gave him a thoughtful look and set her glass down. "More like cheese mixed with mud."

He peered at the label and grimaced. "Earthflower," he muttered. "What the hell does that even mean?"

Ellie smiled, then reached out and rested a hand on his. "I'm sorry, Ty. For everything you went through as a kid. For the things you're probably not even telling me. Not that you have to—I know we're only sleeping together, but it means a lot that you shared that with me just now."

Something knocked against the tender edges of his gut, and it wasn't the kombucha. It was the warm sympathy in Ellie's eyes and the softness in her voice. It was the slow, subtle shifting of the walls he'd built to protect his stupid, battered heart.

"Thank you," he murmured, meeting her eyes again. Their startling blueness made his breath snag in his lungs. Ty cleared his throat. "How about you?"

"What about me?" Ellie shifted in her chair, bumping his knee with hers. Ty wanted to reach out and stroke her bare leg, but he focused on keeping his hands to himself. He wasn't experienced with conversations like this, but something told him groping her wasn't the right approach.

"What's your reason for just wanting a casual fling instead of happily-ever-after?"

Ellie laughed, but there was a flicker of something in her eyes. Sadness, maybe. He wanted to understand why someone like Ellie Sanders, who could have any man she wanted, would be in a sex-only relationship.

"Well," she said, giving a small shrug as she looked down into her glass. "I already tried the whole happily-ever-after mess. It didn't exactly go like the fairy tales."

"So, you're giving up?"

"I'm not a quitter," she said. "I have a successful career, a healthy son, hobbies I love—"

"I didn't say you were a quitter," Ty said, smiling a little to let her know he hadn't meant anything bad. "I just wondered why you weren't interested in trying again with relationships or love or—whatever."

"Are you?" She gave him a pointed look, holding his gaze a few beats longer than he'd expected. He understood that she wasn't asking if he was interested in a relationship with *her*. She was talking about the bigger picture.

"No," he said. "I've had enough disappointment to last a lifetime, thanks."

She smiled. "So, it sounds like we're in the same place."

"Right." Ty nodded, part of him wishing they didn't have heartbreak in common. That things could be different for them.

Ellie looked away first, picking up both glasses of kombucha to empty them into the Big Gulp cup. She popped open a third bottle and dumped the contents into the wineglasses, then nudged one in front of him.

She picked hers up and took a sip, then made a face. "Ugh. Apricots and mustard with a hint of beef jerky."

Ty snorted and turned the bottle around to study the label. "Spring Essence."

"Yuck." Still, she held up her glass and gave him a hopeful look. "Well, Ty. Things haven't gone the way either of us expected in life. I think that's pretty clear."

"Right," he said, and tried to swallow back the lump in his throat.

"But cheers to having fun with each other anyway."

"Cheers."

He picked up his glass and clinked it against hers with an unidentifiable ache in his chest. He wasn't sure what to call it, but he was sure about one thing.

He was falling for Ellie Sanders.

• • •

A week later, Ellie was in the kitchen with Miriam, putting the finishing touches on a lasagna for dinner. Jason had taken Henry with him to the hardware store to pick up some more plumbing supplies, leaving the two women alone to drink grape juice out of Ellie's best wineglasses.

"If I swirl the glass and don't sniff too deeply, I can alretend it's Bordeaux," Miriam said.

"Just a few more weeks." Ellie gave a supportive nod and laid the last noodle atop the thick mound of spinach and ricotta and Italian sausage. "It'll all be worth it, I promise."

"I can't see my toes." Miriam peered toward her feet with a forlorn expression. "Are they still down there?"

"Yep," Ellie assured her as she spread a handful of shredded cheese over the top of the casserole dish. "Your shoes even match."

"That's a relief," Miriam said. "Jason had to help me put them on this morning. I could be wearing soccer cleats for all I know."

"They're very cute ballet flats," Ellie said. "Green ones."

"To go with my blue skirt," Miriam muttered. "Leave it to

my husband to dress me in Seattle Seahawks colors."

"You look great."

Miriam grinned and plucked a carrot stick from a bowl on the counter, pausing to swirl it in a bowl of ranch dip. "So, things are still going well with Ty?"

Ellie had wondered how long it would take for the inquisition to start. "Yeah," she said, doing her best to sound nonchalant. "Thanks again for keeping Henry the other night."

"Hey, anything to give you a shot at a sexy sleepover." Miriam leaned back against the counter and took a sip of grape juice, then made a face.

"He didn't actually sleep over," Ellie pointed out. "I was worried about Henry being just down the street and needing to come home early for some reason."

Miriam rolled her eyes. "Hon. You know I wouldn't do that to you. I'd have locked the kid in a closet before I'd let him come barging in on your sexy times."

"Remind me never to let you watch him again."

Miriam laughed and grabbed another carrot stick. "I thought it was sweet watching Ty with him," she said. "Jason's been the only guy in Henry's life for so long. It's good for him to see grown men come in all shapes and sizes and personalities."

"I'm not looking to Ty to be a father figure," Ellie said. "I'm not even sure how much I should have them around each other."

"What do you mean?"

"What if Henry gets attached?"

"It's not like you're introducing him to Henry as his future stepdad," Miriam pointed out. "He's mommy's friend. Mommy has plenty of friends, and it's good for him to see they can be any gender."

"I guess so." Ellie focused on making a foil tent over

the lasagna to keep the cheese from burning. She didn't like admitting that she'd pictured the stepfather scenario a time or two in the last week.

Like when she'd opened another shitty letter from her ex. Chuck had gone on for ten pages about all the reasons she should ignore the state-mandated child support requirements and cut him some slack. She'd stared at the words a long time, wondering how he managed a hundred paragraphs about his money woes, but hadn't managed a birthday card when Henry turned six.

Instead of responding, she'd crumpled the pages and shoved them into the recycling bin. No matter how much it had stung when Chuck decided not to be part of her life, it hurt ten times more knowing he didn't want to be part of Henry's.

*All the more reason you shouldn't get too attached to Ty,* she reminded herself. *No one should have to go through that again.*

Miriam grabbed another carrot from the bowl next to Ellie, jarring her back to the moment. "How did dinner go Tuesday?" she asked. "You said Ty was coming over?"

"Yeah," she admitted, smiling a little as she remembered how sweet he'd been with Henry, bringing him a pair of Batman sunglasses that made the boy whoop and shriek with joy.

"I like spending time with him," Ellie admitted.

"He seems to like you, too."

*Like.* Is that all this was? Things had seemed a little muddy lately, and Ellie felt hopelessly out of practice. Did casual hookups bring gifts to your kid? Did friends-with-benefits text you at night to make sure you made it home safely from your Madame Butterfly sales party? She had no idea, but Ty Hendrix was a good guy. A guy she liked a helluva lot more than she'd expected to.

Ellie's phone rang on the counter beside her, and she glanced at the screen.

*Ty Hendrix*, the readout said, making Ellie wonder if she'd summoned him with her thoughts. She reached for the phone while Miriam gave her a knowing look and sipped her grape juice. "Hey, Ty," Ellie said as breezily as possible. "What's up?"

"I was just thinking about you," he said. "You and Henry."

"Oh?" She picked up the lasagna and headed toward the oven, determined not to read too much into his entrée to conversation. Miriam turned and opened the oven door for her, and Ellie slid the dish inside and pushed the door shut with her hip.

"Yeah," Ty continued. "Speak Up just got a new RFP for Great Wolf Lodge, so it made me think of you guys."

"I know what Great Wolf Lodge is," she said. "It's that big water park in Washington that I'm always hearing about from other moms. But what's an RFP?"

"Request for Proposal," he said. "They want a bid on some video work. TV commercials, some things to embed on their website. Promotional stuff."

"That sounds exciting."

"Yeah, it is." Ty cleared his throat, and Ellie wondered if he was nervous about something. "I was hoping to submit a rough video with the proposal. Something to give them an idea what we can do."

"Seems like a smart idea."

"Yeah. I thought I'd do a little filming at the park. Spend some time checking out the waterslides and pools and things like that."

Ellie set the timer on the oven, intrigued by the tense edge to Ty's voice. What was on his mind? "I've heard great things about the place," she said. "That sounds fun."

"You know what sounds like even more fun? If you and Henry came with me."

"To Great Wolf Lodge?" Ellie dropped her oven mitt on the floor. Miriam made a halfhearted attempt to grab it, then gave up, resting her juice-filled wineglass on her belly. "That's a couple of hours away."

"I think Henry would love it," Ty continued. "Maybe it would make up for the disappointment over the paycheck thing."

"That was really a non-issue, Ty."

He cleared his throat again, and Ellie got the sense he wasn't convinced. "Well, anyway, I think it would be a kick," he said. "Now that you've mastered your camera shyness, I was hoping you'd let me use you for a little footage."

"You mean filming us? Henry and me?"

"Yes. Exactly, yes." His anxiousness made sense now, and something about that charmed her. "It would save me the hassle of hiring models or getting releases signed at the park."

Ellie stepped back from the oven, not sure how to read his invitation. "So, this is a work trip?"

Miriam quirked an eyebrow at her, but Ellie looked away, doing her best to stay cool. She grabbed a rag from the sink and began wiping down the counter.

"Work and pleasure," he said. "I don't mean *pleasure* pleasure," he added quickly. "The company offered to comp us one of their Grizzly Bear Suites, so everyone would have a separate bed to themselves. You, Henry, me —"

He trailed off there, and Ellie smiled because he'd thought this through so thoroughly. "When did you want to go?"

The relief in his voice was practically palpable. "So, you're up for it?"

"Of course. You're right; Henry would love it, He's seen commercials for the place, but I've always told him it's too expensive."

"Are you free this weekend?"

"I think so," she said, wondering if she had a bathing suit

that would be presentable for something like this. She'd have to go shopping. Henry probably needed new swim trunks, too, and maybe she ought to lose a few pounds before —

"Ellie?"

"Yeah?"

"I'm really excited about taking this trip with you," he said.

Ellie gripped the phone tighter, grateful he couldn't see the big, goofy smile plastered on her face. "Me, too."

They said their good-byes and hung up, with Ellie still grinning like an idiot. The second she set the phone down, Miriam pounced.

"I knew it!" Miriam said.

"What?" Ellie bent to pick up the oven mitt, doing her best to look nonchalant. She went back to wiping a section of counter that was already spotless.

"I knew Ty had a reason for wanting that RFP." Miriam grinned and popped a carrot stick in her mouth. "He likes you. And Henry, too, of course."

"He just wants people to be in the footage," she said. "So he doesn't have to get model releases signed."

Miriam laughed like that was the funniest thing she'd heard in years. Shaking her head, she set her grape juice on the counter. "Honey. There are three other videographers under him who would have gladly taken the project. Every single one of them has kids of their own."

Ellie looked at her, startled. "So, he could have pawned this off on someone else?"

"Most certainly. The man's smitten."

"The man's getting free sex," Ellie said, then frowned. "Actually, I guess that's not true. Not on this trip, anyway. Apparently, he booked us some fancy suite where we'll each have our own room."

Miriam grinned. "He wants to spend time with you, no

sex required. I think you've got yourself a relationship."

Ellie shook her head, even as her heart tilted a little at the thought of it. Was this turning into something more than a hookup?

Did she really want that?

"I don't think so," Ellie said, even as the flutter in her belly built to something more like rippling waves. Was it possible? No, of course not. But maybe —

"I do love spending time with him," she admitted.

"He's a great guy." Miriam eyed her with a serious expression. "I would have chased him away from you weeks ago if that weren't true."

Ellie smiled and adjusted the dials on the oven. Was it possible for a fling to turn into something else? Was there any chance Ty might want that?

"I didn't want to like him this much." The second she'd blurted the words, heat flooded her cheeks. She might as well have confessed to peering through the men's room door or something.

But Miriam only laughed and grabbed another carrot stick. "Believe me, honey — I know exactly what that's like."

She turned to her sister-in-law, keenly aware that Miriam did know. She'd had her own reasons for not wanting to fall for Jason. Reasons that involved a past heartache not so different from Ellie's.

"Should I say anything?" Ellie asked. "I mean — I don't even know if I want more than a fling, so it seems stupid to just blurt out what I'm feeling without knowing if he's on the same page." She bit her lip, softening her voice a little. "I don't want anyone getting hurt."

Her throat tightened as she remembered the flicker of Chuck's taillights the night he drove away, the way it left her empty and aching and determined to never fall in love again. It was the same hollowness she'd seen in Ty's eyes when he talked about losing his grandma.

She remembered that kind of pain. They both did.

"You deserve to be happy, El." Miriam gave her a knowing look, and Ellie wondered if her sister-in-law had read her mind. "Ty's been making you happy, right?"

"Right." A flush of pleasure rushed up her arms, and she caught herself smiling like a big, dopey dork.

Miriam smiled back, not unfamiliar with Ellie's dorkiness. "So why not take a chance?"

*Why not?* The question pinged around in Ellie's brain, giving her zaps of joy and terror and everything in between.

"Maybe." Ellie bent down to check the oven, hoping the heat of it would mask her burning cheeks. Hoping like hell she wasn't wishing for something that would break her heart again.

# Chapter Twelve

Ty stepped into the indoor waterpark, overwhelmed by the smell of chlorine, the shrieks of small children, and an intense wave of bewildered fondness coursing through him. Was this really his life?

"Whoa." Henry stared in awe at the spectacle before them. His gaze swung from the wave park to the massive play structure spurting water from colorful pipes. As Ty looked on, the boy studied the families playing water basketball in the far pool before he pivoted to survey huge bank of water slides in the corner. A family of five emerged laughing from the end of the tube, swirling through the landing pool in a burst of cheers and a bright yellow raft.

When he looked up at Ty, Henry's small face was glowing. "Can we go on everything?"

"Whatever you want," Ty assured him. "Your wristband lets you use all the park amenities."

"As long as you're tall enough," Ellie added. "We need to check the rules, first."

"Right," Ty said. He needed to remember Henry was a

child. "The rules are there to keep you safe."

"Okay," Henry said, watching as another small boy ran past with an ice cream cone. "Where do we start?"

"Let's find a table and put our stuff down," Ellie said. "Maybe someplace close to the bathrooms."

Ty nodded, amazed that she always seemed to think of everything. She wore a conservative red one-piece that tied behind her neck, showcasing those gorgeous collarbones and the swell at the tops of her breasts. It wasn't flashy or revealing, but something about the modesty of the suit made it even more appealing. God, she was beautiful. Her blond hair was pulled back in a low ponytail, and she wore some kind of flowy skirt thing knotted at one hip.

She caught him staring at her and smiled. "What?"

"You're amazing." He cleared his throat, hoping that didn't sound too sentimental. "I'm glad you agreed to let me film you."

"Thanks for helping me with my camera shyness," she said. "And I'm glad you brought us here. This looks fun."

It *did*. If someone had told Ty six months ago that he'd be giddy about hanging out at a family-friendly water park, he would have laughed his ass off. But he'd looked forward to this getaway all week.

"Come on," he said. "Let's grab a table."

They made their way to the other side of the space, headed for an empty table between the two locker rooms. Ellie set down her beach bag, while Ty began unpacking his video equipment. He'd decided to keep things simple, skipping the lighting and just working with a small handheld camera. If they got the job, he'd bring out all the best stuff from his studio. He'd hire real models, too, though it was hard to imagine any mother/son duo more adorable than Ellie and Henry.

While the two of them chatted beside him, Ty glanced

around, assessing the lighting and deciding what would look best on camera. Small kids laughed and shrieked with joy as their parents chased them through sprinklers. So this is what a happy childhood was like.

"You hafta take your shirt off."

Henry's small voice startled Ty at first, and he looked down to see the six-year-old regarding him with a serious expression. "Boys don't wear shirts at the pool," Henry advised him. "Only girls do, because they hafta cover up their boobies."

"Breasts," Ellie said. "We use proper words for body parts, remember?"

"Breasts," Henry repeated, nodding. "Come on, Mommy. Take off your skirt, and Ty takes off his shirt and then we can all go in the water."

Ellie shot a nervous glance at Ty. Her gaze flicked to the spot over his heart, covered at the moment by his gray T-shirt. She mouthed a two-syllable word at him, and it took Ty a few beats to figure out what she was trying to say.

"Oh," he said, realization dawning. He grinned and grabbed the hem of his shirt, then tugged it over his head and tossed it aside.

Henry frowned and pointed at the large waterproof bandage Ty had placed over the Johnny Cash tattoo. "You have an owie?"

Ellie's face flushed with relief, and she pointed at the towering water feature in the center of the space. "What do you say we check that out, sweetie?" she said to Henry, saving Ty from having to explain. "We can walk around for a few minutes so Ty has a chance to get his equipment ready."

"Yeah!" Henry scampered forward, leaving his mother behind.

She smiled at Ty then leaned closer. "Thank you," she whispered. "You're such a good guy."

The compliment made Ty's throat tighten, and all he could do was nod. "I figured it was best to keep it covered," he said.

"Smart thinking."

Ty smiled as relief washed through him. Okay, so maybe he didn't always know about things like car seats and child-friendly snacks and the importance of not saying things a kid might take literally and be disappointed.

But he'd had the foresight to cover his profane tattoo. Maybe that was a sign of something.

Ellie scurried after Henry, her ponytail swishing as she moved. God, what a woman. She joined Henry at the base of the play structure, pointing up to where a bucket the size of a small car seemed to tip precariously to one side. Water poured from it in sheets, and a small herd of children squealed with delight as they scampered in the downpour.

Joy bubbled hot and raw in Ty's chest as he watched Ellie and Henry dance through a row of small geysers jetting up from the skid-proof floor. He had to remind himself to focus on lighting and angles instead of how beautiful she was in her red swimsuit with her ponytail shimmering with water droplets.

Turning his attention back to his equipment, he took out his Nikon and made some adjustments. He glanced up to see Ellie and Henry swooping through the spray of a large geyser now, with Henry waving his hands and whooping with glee. That joy-tinged voice was as familiar now as his own heartbeat, and maybe as vital. Ellie skipped behind her son, the happiness on her face so pure, so lovely, that Ty flicked "record" on his camera and stole a few quick seconds of video.

His chest ached with something between longing and happiness, a feeling he'd never had in his whole life.

*Don't get attached. Don't get attached.*

"Too late," he murmured softly.

Then he looped the camera around his neck and strode

forward to join them.

• • •

Four hours later, Ty clicked off his camera and set it down on the table. He reached for a slice of pepperoni pizza, glad he'd thought to grab extra napkins.

"I can't believe I just let you film me in a bathing suit with cheese hanging out of my mouth," Ellie said, grinning at him as she wiped her hands on a napkin. "You've clearly conquered my camera shyness."

He reached over and dabbed a fleck of tomato sauce from the corner of her lip, then smiled back at her. "I promise not to put anything in the video that would be embarrassing to you," he said. "Thanks again for being such a good sport about this."

"Thank *you* for bringing us here," she said, shooting Henry a meaningful look.

The boy nodded as he finished wolfing down his slice of pizza. "Yeah," he said. "Thank you, Mr. Ty."

"You're welcome, Mr. Henry."

The boy grinned then looked at his mother. "Can I go back in the water now?"

"Only if you stay right here on that big tree-fort thing where I can see you," she said. "Let's keep out of the pools for now."

"Okay!" He started to scramble off, but Ellie caught him by the arm and wiped his face with a napkin. "There," she said, giving him a big, smacky kiss on the cheek that made Ty wonder what life would have been like if his mother hadn't died. He barely remembered her, but wanted to believe she might have been something like Ellie.

He'd only met Anna's mom a couple of times, and mostly he remembered the smell of cigarette smoke and an air of disdain. She'd barely wanted to be saddled with her own daughter, let alone some grubby kid who looked just like his jailbird father.

"Thanks again, Ty."

Ellie's voice jarred him back to the present. "For lunch, or for inviting you here?"

"All of it," she said with a laugh. "But I was actually talking about this." She touched a finger to the waterproof bandage that masked his Johnny Cash tattoo. "I'd never ask you to cover it, but I appreciate that you thought to do it."

"Yeah," he said, feeling a twinge of pride. "I figured hundreds of small children didn't need to be flipped off by a country music legend at a water park."

She smiled and picked a slice of pepperoni off the half-eaten slice of pizza abandoned on Henry's plate. "What's the story behind it, anyway?" she asked. "If you don't mind me asking."

He shrugged, not sure how much to volunteer. "Johnny Cash was my dad's favorite singer," he said. "Sometimes my dad even pretended to be him. It was one of his favorite scams."

"I see," Ellie said, nodding as she nibbled the pepperoni slice. "So you got the tattoo to…honor him?"

He realized she was fumbling for the right word, but that wasn't it at all. Not even close. "No." Ty snorted with disgust. "To remind me where I come from."

He stopped himself there, not wanting to put a damper on the afternoon. Not wanting to complete the rest of that thought.

*To remind me that I don't want to be like him.*

He cleared his throat and decided to change the subject. "How have the new videos been performing on your website?"

Ellie grinned and wiped her hands on a napkin. "Really great," she said. "I've heard from so many clients who love seeing them. You were right about women wanting that educational component."

"I'm glad." Ty glanced over at the big water tower where Henry was playing with a group of boys who looked a year or two older than him. He was laughing and splashing and having a great time. The elation in their little faces was enough to coax a smile from him, too.

He glanced at Ellie to see her watching her boy with such love in her eyes it took Ty's breath away.

"He's a good kid," Ty said.

"Thanks." She looked back at him and smiled. "I think I'll keep him." She balled up the napkin and glanced over her shoulder toward the locker rooms. "Actually, would you mind watching him for just a few minutes? I need to use the restroom."

"Um, sure." Ty gulped back a wave of panic, then realized he should probably try to sound more confident. "No problem." He glanced around, a little frantic at the idea of being left in charge. Okay, so there were at least a million lifeguards patrolling the place, and Henry wasn't anywhere near any of the pools.

*You can do this.*

"I'll keep an eye on him."

"Thanks." Ellie got up and headed for the locker room. Ty admired the sway of her hips.

*Stop ogling the mom and keep your eyes on the kid, jackass.*

He turned and looked back at the play structure, momentarily alarmed not to see Henry. As his heart began to race, he scanned the walkways and stairs for a sign of the familiar blond head.

A female shriek snapped his attention to a spot just below one of the bridges. A woman stood clutching her top, staring up at the buckets of water pouring down on her. She was laughing, but another set of giggles echoed from above.

*Henry.* Ty stood up and headed toward the bridge.

As he mounted the skid-proof stairs, three older boys scurried away, leaving Henry alone on the bridge with his hands clutching one of the yellow buckets.

"Hey, little man," Ty said. "Whatcha doing?"

Henry looked up and grinned. "My new friends showed me a good trick," he said.

"What's that?" Ty ambled up beside him and leaned against the railing. He had a pretty good idea what the trick was. Maybe his childhood hadn't included waterparks, but he'd been a six-year-old boy once.

"If you get the buckets all full of water and then wait, you can pour them on the ladies underneath," Henry explained.

"I see," Ty said slowly, admiring the thought process even though the moment called for something other than a high-five. "And why would you want to do that?"

"Because sometimes I get to see their boobies."

Well. Couldn't fault that logic.

Ty cleared his throat. Ellie wouldn't be a fan of the boy using slang instead of real words, but that wasn't Ty's chief concern.

"How do you think the ladies feel about that?" he asked. He kept his voice casual, not wanting to be the asshole scolding a kid who wasn't his, but still. Something had to be said, and he was the grown-up who happened to be standing here.

Henry frowned, looking mystified. He glanced down as though expecting a bikini-clad lady to appear and provide the answer.

"I don't know," Henry said. "Most of them laugh."

"Right." Ty repositioned himself against the railing beside Henry, edging sideways to let a family move past them on the bridge. "Sometimes people laugh when they're uncomfortable, though. Have you ever done that?"

"Maybe," Henry said, sounding uncertain. His lashes were flecked with water droplets, and Ty wondered how much booby action the boy actually saw without his glasses.

"I'm going to tell you a secret," Ty said. "Are you ready?"

The boy's eyes lit up, and he nodded like Ty had just offered him a case of Butterfingers. "Yeah!"

"Okay, but this secret is just for gentlemen. Are you a gentleman?"

"Like Gentleman Ghost from Batman?"

Ty frowned, not sure what the hell the kid was talking about. "Maybe. Is Gentleman Ghost a good guy or a bad guy?"

"A bad guy."

"Oh. Then no. Not like him." Ty rubbed a hand over his chin, pretty sure he was messing this up. "A good guy gentleman is someone who's kind to ladies," he said. "To all people, really, but especially to ladies."

"How come?" Henry asked.

*So it'll earn you a fine piece of ass*, growled his father's voice in the back of his head.

But Ty shoved it aside, determined to do a better job of this than his old man had. "Because it's the right thing to do," he said. "A gentleman tries not to do things to make ladies uncomfortable," he said. "Like trying to look at their boobi—at their *breasts* when they don't want that."

"Oh," said Henry, sounding genuinely thoughtful.

"A gentleman does kind things instead," he said. "Like holding doors open for ladies and saying please and thank you."

"And keeping my pirate parts to myself," Henry added.

"What?"

Henry nodded, his expression serious. "I told the babysitter I had a penis, and Uncle Jason said I needed to keep my pirate parts to myself."

"Oh." Ty nodded, doing his best not to laugh. "Right. Your private parts. You should definitely keep those to yourself."

Ty scanned the waterpark to find Ellie striding back to where she'd left him, brow furrowing as she saw the table abandoned. He waved an arm, trying to catch her eye as a group of giggling kids hurried past. When she spotted him, she broke into a smile. She started toward then, damp blond ponytail trailing behind her

Feeling warm all over, Ty looked down at Henry. "So does all that make sense to you?"

Henry nodded and wiped a trail of water off his cheek. "Yes," he said. "I would like to learn how to be a gentleman," he said. "The nice kind, not the ghost kind or the bad guy kind. I want to be a *good* gentleman."

As Ellie emerged up the ladder, Ty let his gaze drift over the droplets of water glistening on the tops of her breasts. He ordered himself to knock it off, dragging his gaze to her face instead.

"You and me both, kid," he said. "You and me both."

# Chapter Thirteen

"Thanks again, Ty," Ellie whispered that night after they'd tucked Henry in. The boy was sleeping soundly in his little bunk designed to look like a bear den.

Ty and Ellie had snuggled up on the suite's sofa to enjoy a glass of wine before retiring to their separate beds for the night.

For Ty, it was pretty much the perfect end to a perfect day. Jesus. How the hell had that happened?

"You truly thought of everything," Ellie continued, tucking her bare feet up under her as she took a small sip of wine. "The sleeping arrangements, the snacks, the tattoo cover-up. For a guy who's never been around kids, you're doing a pretty amazing job."

He took a sip of wine to mask his smile, not wanting to admit how deliriously proud those words made him. "Maybe I'm getting the hang of it," he said. "I know I love spending time with you. Both of you," he added.

"Henry's a great kid." Ellie didn't bother covering her own smile, which charmed the hell out of him. She wore no makeup at all, and her hair was damp from the shower. Even the orange plastic bracelet she wore to mark her as a lodge guest seemed cheery and festive on her lovely, delicate wrist. Ty reached for her hand, planting a soft kiss on the palm before setting it back to rest on her knee.

"You're a great mom." In all his life, Ty never thought that would be something he'd find attractive in a woman. He leaned close and brushed a kiss across her lips before sitting back against the sofa.

"And I love that you make me feel like more than just a mom," Ellie murmured. "You make me feel like a woman." She winced and shook her head, then took a sip of her wine. "God, that sounded cheesy."

"Not at all," he said. "I know what you mean."

She smiled at him and moved her hand on his knee. It felt good there, like it belonged. Like *he* belonged. Not bad for a foster kid who'd never been part of a real family.

His chest ached suddenly, and Ty took another sip of wine. "Ellie," he said slowly. "Can we talk about us?"

Alarm flashed in her eyes, but her smile stayed frozen in place. She stiffened beside him, though, and she took a moment before nodding. "Sure. What did you want to talk about?"

He took a deep breath, hoping he wasn't about to make an ass of himself. Hoping they were on the same page. "I know we agreed this was just a casual hookup," he said. "That neither of us wanted a relationship."

"Right," Ellie said slowly, giving him a wary look. "That *is* what we agreed."

"But I've been thinking I might want more than that." Ty's heart was pounding in his head, and he forced himself not to glance away—to keep staring straight into those blue eyes as he put himself on the line and put those words out there. "And I was wondering if you might feel the same."

• • •

Ellie stared back at Ty, hardly believing her ears. Had he really just suggested a relationship? Like an actual, honest-to-God relationship?

She found herself nodding, a little numb from the shock. But mixed in with the shock was something a lot like joy. "Yes," she said. "I think I might like that, too."

Until that moment, she hadn't admitted how much she wanted more. She hadn't allowed herself to think that way, convinced they needed to keep things casual. Convinced she couldn't go down that path again.

But the more she'd gotten to know Ty, the more she realized she'd like to give it a shot. Knowing he wanted that, too, was like a big, fizzy pleasure bubble swelling in the center of her chest.

"I'm a little out of practice," she said. "At relationships, I mean. My last one didn't end well, and I probably have trust issues."

Ty smiled and reached up to tuck a lock of hair behind her ear. "Thanks for the warning," he said. "If it makes you feel better, I'm a bit of a commitment-phobe."

"Really?" A trickle of unease moved through her veins, but she pushed it aside. If he was admitting it, maybe that proved he wouldn't be like Chuck. That he wouldn't cut and run at the first sign of trouble.

"My childhood—uh—wasn't so great." He seemed to hesitate, and Ellie felt a flutter of sympathy. "You know that already. But I just mean I didn't have the greatest example of family life growing up, so that part is going to be kinda new to me."

Ellie nodded, grateful that he was willing to lay it out for her up front. She and Chuck had never done that.

"I'm a hypochondriac," Ellie said, needing to put that out there. "Everyone I love gets marched straight to the doctor at the first sign of a sniffle."

"Understandable," he said. He took a sip of his wine,

looking pensive.

"What else?" Ellie asked. "Do you have any more issues you want to disclose?"

Ty gave a grim nod. "I hog the covers."

She stifled the urge to laugh. "I did notice that our first night." She lifted her glass and took a small sip. The wine was plummy and earthy and gave her a blissful heat in the middle of her belly. She snuggled closer to Ty on the couch, resting the glass on her knee as she regarded her new boyfriend with a small smile.

*Boyfriend.*

The smile got bigger. "I can live with the bed hogging," she said. Twirling the glass on the knee of her yoga pants, she considered her own list of faults. What else did Ty need to know about her before signing on for a real relationship?

"I bite my nails," she said. "I've tried for years to kick the habit, but I can't. It drove my ex-husband nuts when we'd be sitting on the couch together watching TV."

Ty lifted one eyebrow. "That's the definition of a first world problem." He scratched his chin with a thoughtful expression. "Um, I'm allergic to cats," he said. "If things got serious between us and we wanted to move in together, we couldn't ever have one."

"Good to know," Ellie said, formulating a future in her mind that included a cover-hogging, feline-free existence. It wasn't so bad. "I'm a horrible singer," she admitted. "But I love to sing in the shower and in the car."

"I can be a jerk until I've had my first cup of coffee."

She grinned. "I hate coffee. I'm a tea drinker." She set a hand on his knee, delighted to be touching him. To be sitting here with him, getting this all out in the open, disclosing all the landmines.

"I'm a control freak with the television remote," he said.

"I'm a night owl," she said. "And I know you're an early riser. I'm going to piss you off at some point by staying up too late and wanting to sleep in."

"Doubtful," he said. "I'm a workout junkie. I get cranky if I don't make it to the gym at least five days a week."

Ellie smiled and leaned into one impressive bicep. "I can live with that." She sipped her wine and tried to think of more personal faults. "I lose my sunglasses constantly," she said. "I go through at least twenty pairs a year."

"I'll buy you new ones." Ty grinned down at her then rested his wineglass on the end table. "So now that we've laid all that out there, is this where we decide if we can live with each other's least admirable traits?"

"I think so."

Ty smiled. "Sign me up."

"Yeah?"

"Definitely. You?"

Ellie nodded, feeling giddy and joyful and only a little bit scared of what this all meant. "I'm game if you are."

He picked up his glass and clinked it against hers. "Well, okay then." He leaned in to kiss her, then drew back and looked her in the eye. "We're in a relationship."

Ellie set her wine down then pulled him against her for a hug. He was big and strong and solid and warm, and most of her felt pretty sure this was a great idea. "Thanks, Ty."

"For what?"

"For being brave enough to start that conversation," she said. "For being such a great guy."

Something flashed in his eyes, but he nodded and smiled and stroked a finger over her cheek. "I'll do my best to be a great guy for you," he said. "For you and for Henry."

She smiled and kissed him again, trying not to notice the fear in his eye.

Trying not to think there was something they'd failed to disclose. Something they'd overlooked that could bring this whole thing crashing down.

# Chapter Fourteen

"Will I get to watch myself on the television?"

At the sound of Henry's voice from the backseat, Ty glanced in the rearview mirror. The boy was still wearing his fuzzy gray wolf-ear headband from Great Wolf Lodge and a smudge of chocolate on one cheek.

The grin on his face made Ty smile, too. "You mean the video I was shooting of you at the waterpark?" Ty asked.

"Yeah," Henry said. "Will it be a movie on a screen like when Mommy and me went to see *Finding Dory* and I got popcorn and Skittles, or will it be on TV like *Batman: the Brave and the Bold* when Uncle Jason makes us chocolate milkshakes?"

Ty smiled, charmed by the idea that the joy in Henry's world revolved around snacks and family relations. He glanced at Ellie in the passenger seat, and his heart gave a pleasant twist. Her window was cracked just a little, making her blond hair ripple in the breeze. He was driving a station wagon, a rental car he'd picked up for the business trip and because he wanted something kid-friendly. The whole arrangement felt so comfortable and domestic that Ty reached over and squeezed her hand.

As Ellie smiled in response, Ty turned back to answer Henry's question. "Well, first I have to take all my footage and edit it," he explained. "Do you know what edit means?"

Henry frowned, his small face scrunching up in the rearview mirror. "Mommy told Uncle Jason I need to learn to edit myself in public," he said. "And Uncle Jason said sometimes a guy's gotta burp. So, I think edit means you cover your mouth."

Ellie stifled a giggle beside him. Struggling to keep a straight face, he gave a quick nod. "I like your powers of deduction," he said. "It's a little like that. The idea of figuring out how to work with what you've got. It's about looking at the good stuff and the bad stuff and all the stuff in the middle, and making the very best of it. Does that make sense?"

Henry nodded and pushed his glasses up his nose, shifting a little in his booster seat. "I think so. Hey, can we get a hamburger?"

Ellie snorted in the passenger seat and glanced over her shoulder at her son. "Way to keep up with the conversation, buddy."

Ty laughed and glanced at the clock on the dashboard. "He does have a point. It's almost dinnertime."

He hesitated, wondering whether to suggest a drive-thru or if Ellie was one of those moms who never let her kid eat fast food. Seemed wise to play it safe.

"My place is on the south end of town," he murmured to her, trying to keep his voice low in case she didn't like the plan. No sense getting Henry's hopes up. "I could have us there and have burgers on the grill in fifteen minutes if you're interested."

Ellie shot him a grateful look. "That would be amazing. I have nothing at home to cook. Besides, it'll be fun to see where you live."

He smiled at her, amazed at how normal this all seemed. How easy it was to have a real relationship.

*I have a girlfriend.* The words filled him with excitement instead of fear, which was a miracle.

Okay, so there was a tiny bit of dread in there. But he was working on it.

They'd agreed that for now, they wouldn't use terms like "boyfriend" or "girlfriend" around Henry, or give him any reason to ask questions about the nature of the relationship or where it was headed.

In his short span of time with Henry, Ty had grown to appreciate the need to speak with discretion around a chatty, inquisitive six-year-old.

But he and Ellie had agreed the occasional G-rated display of affection was fine, so Ty reached over and gave her knee a squeeze. She looked at him and smiled, then glanced down at her phone. Her brow furrowed as she read the words on the screen. He didn't mean to snoop, but he thought he saw the name "Chuck" at the top.

He glanced back at the road, trying to remember if that was her ex-husband's name. The thought of her staying connected with Henry's dad didn't bother him, but the worry on her face did.

He glanced back to see her biting her lip.

*You okay?* he mouthed.

Ellie shook her head and frowned, then gave a faint head-tilt toward the backseat. *His father,* she mouthed. *Money.*

Ty's blood turned icy. She'd filled him in on the asshole's persistent requests to lower his child support, and how tired she was of all the arm-twisting.

It made Ty so angry he wanted to punch something.

But as he pulled off the exit and headed toward his house, he told himself to keep his cool. "I think I have apples and some celery in my fridge," he said loudly for Henry's benefit. "So we're all set with the fruits and veggies."

"My hero," Ellie said, beaming at him.

It hurt his heart a little to think her idea of heroism involved fresh produce. She deserved so much more than that. So did Henry, for that matter.

As Ty pulled into his driveway, he said a silent prayer he'd picked up all his dirty laundry off the floor and hadn't left any *Playboy* magazines lying around. He was pretty sure he'd tidied up before hitting the road, so hopefully there'd be no surprises.

"Here we are," he announced as he pulled into the driveway. He thought about pulling into the garage, but his truck was already in there, and the floor was littered with motorcycle parts. The front entrance was more scenic, anyway. He studied it with a critical eye, wondering how the cozy rambler looked to her. His place was small but tidy, with a manicured front yard and a big oak tree in front.

The realtor had patted his arm when he'd bought the place five years ago. "That's the perfect place for a tree fort, don't you think?"

Ty—who couldn't fathom needing a tree fort for any reason—had nodded and changed the subject.

Now, he was looking at the tree with renewed interest.

"Your place is adorable," Ellie said. "Did you plant those daisies?"

He shook his head, liking the idea that she saw him as the sort of guy who'd plant daisies. Maybe he could be.

"They were here when I moved in." He unbuckled his seat belt and pushed open the door, prompting her to do the same. "Let's leave your bags out here, and I'll run you guys home after dinner."

Ellie got out of the car, looking a little nervous as she followed him up the walk. Henry fell into step beside her, reaching for his mother's hand. Ty unlocked the door and ushered them inside, relieved the place didn't smell like a bachelor pad.

"Can I get you something to drink?" he asked, bemused to find himself in the role of a host. "I have water, milk, soda—"

"Milk would be great," Ellie said. "For both of us."

"I would like chocolate in mine," Henry piped.

Ty hesitated. "I'm not sure if I have any—"

"Plain milk would be fine," Ellie said, giving Henry a stern look. "You know better than to ask for sweets without permission."

"Sorry, Mommy."

"It's okay." Ellie ruffled his hair, while Ty stood watching, struck once more by how many landmines there were in interactions with children. Sweets and caffeine and privileges and rules—it was all so foreign to him, and there were a million ways to screw this up.

But he focused on pouring the milk, selecting plastic cups in case of accidental droppage. Maybe he could learn this. Maybe he'd figure it out.

Once everyone had a drink, Ty led them outside onto his sunny deck. While he fired up the grill, Ellie got busy wiping down the table and slicing apples and carrots into neat little piles. The whole scene was so domestic that Ty caught himself smiling at the craziness of it all. How much his world had changed in just a few weeks.

He was still smiling as he walked out to the garage to hunt for an old soccer ball.

When he returned to the back deck, he gave the ball a few quick pumps of air and handed to Henry. "You can kick this around the yard if you like."

Henry beamed and shoved his glasses up his nose. "Wanna play with me?"

"I would love to," Ty said, meaning it. "But I need to get the burgers on the grill."

Ellie stood up, nibbling a carrot stick from the tray she'd laid out neatly on Ty's patio table. "I'll play with you, kiddo."

She kicked off her flip-flops then padded, laughing, into the grass. Her blond ponytail streamed behind her as she jogged out into the middle of the yard and assumed an exaggerated goalie stance. "C'mon, buddy! Sock it right here!"

Henry laughed and hustled out into the lawn, booting the ball as hard as possible once he reached it. Ellie scrambled after it barefoot, shouting in triumph as she kicked it back to him. The smell of fresh-cut grass and someone else's barbecue wafted on the breeze as Ty laid the hamburger patties on the grill.

As the meat began to sizzle, Ty's phone buzzed in his pocket. He ignored it, not wanting to interrupt his time with Ellie and Henry to chat with anyone—not wanting to do anything to disturb this perfect evening.

He let the call go to voicemail and turned to flip the burgers. A spatter of hot grease popped, shooting a rocket of gristle backward. It hit his cheek with a searing blast, and Ty dropped the tongs.

"Son of a squirrel fucker!"

He put a hand to his cheek, dimly aware of the silence behind him.

Slowly, he realized the awfulness of what he'd just done. Shoulders tense with shame, Ty turned to see Henry staring open-mouthed with the soccer ball in his hands.

The boy gave him a curious look. "What's a sq—"

"It's nothing, baby," Ellie said, throwing a grimace at Ty. "Come on, toss the ball over here."

"I'm sorry," Ty muttered. He closed his eyes and counted to ten, pissed as hell at himself for screwing this up already. For thinking he could be anything other than a shitty influence on a kid.

With his cheek still stinging, he turned back to the grill and checked the buns. They were toasty enough to serve, so he flipped the burgers one last time and added slices of cheese to each one. Calcium. Kids needed calcium, right?

*You're a fucking joke,* his subconscious chided. *You have no idea what kids need.*

"Dinner's ready!" he called, determined to salvage the evening.

Ellie and Henry hustled over, both gushing about how good everything smelled.

"Here, sweetie," Ellie said, slathering her son's bun with ketchup. "You want pickles this time?"

"No, thank you."

Ty forced a smile, hoping they could all move past his faux pas. "You're so good at that, Henry," he said. "Your manners. I appreciate that you always say please and thank you."

Henry beamed and took a big bite of his burger. "Thank you. I'm trying to be a gentleman. The good kind."

He attempted a conspiratorial wink, but it came out looking more like the effect of a mild stroke.

Ty laughed. "You're welcome."

Ty dove into his own burger, grateful he'd gotten that right. The patty was juicy and flavorful, and the tang of grilled meat made him long for family cookouts he'd never actually experienced.

Henry was halfway through his burger already. Across the table, Ellie was urging him to eat a few carrot slices. Ty picked one up and bit into it, doing his best to set a positive example.

"This is the best hamburger ever," Henry said, wiping his mouth with the back of his hand before Ellie shoved a paper towel napkin at him. "Thank you, Mr. Ty."

"You're welcome, Mr. Henry."

The boy laughed and polished off the last of his burger

before starting in on his apple slices. "Maybe after dinner you'll show me some of the pictures you took today?"

Ty nodded and finished chewing his own mouthful of burger before answering. "Absolutely. We can even run them through the television so it'll be just like watching yourself on a TV show."

Henry's eyes went wide at that suggestion, and he gave an exuberant nod. "And maybe we can put music with it," he said. "Like they do in the movies. Something like nah-nah-nah-nah-nah-nah-nah-nah—"

"Batman!" shouted Ty, completing the song. He held up a hand, delighted when Henry smacked a ketchup-sticky high-five in the center of his palm.

He'd just swallowed his last bite of burger when the doorbell rang. Ty frowned, glancing at his watch.

The screen door to the house was open, and Ellie glanced that direction, holding the last of her burger in both hands. "Are you expecting company?"

"No." Ty swiped at his mouth with a paper towel and pushed back in his chair. "No one ever drops by unannounced. It's probably someone selling something."

"At dinnertime on a Sunday?"

He shrugged and stood up. "I guess it's when they know people are home." As he made his way across the deck, he waved at them to stay seated. "I'll be right back," he called. "Save some apple slices for me."

Henry giggled and pantomimed hiding the plate full of apples. Ellie gave him a mock-stern look and pretended to swat his hand.

The casual playfulness of it all nearly took Ty's breath away.

As the doorbell rang again, Ty hustled through the sliding door and strode through the living room to the front door. Wiping his hands on his shorts, he wondered if this was a teaching opportunity. If Ellie and Henry were watching, maybe this was Ty's chance to show how to be polite but firm with the salesperson, letting them know that while he had the utmost appreciation for small business owners, he wasn't in the market for vacuums or gift wrap or whatever else they were selling.

Ty grabbed the doorknob and twisted, yanking the door open to let in a gust of warm summer breeze. "Evening! Now's actually not a good time for—oh."

The words froze in Ty's throat. He stood staring at the man in the rumpled clothes and grizzled gray beard. A man with worn crinkles at the corners of his eyes and a scowl Ty would know anywhere.

Doffing his dirty, black Johnny Cash cowboy hat, the man stared at him with dark-brown eyes that were achingly familiar.

"Hello, son."

# Chapter Fifteen

Ty stared at his father on his doorstep, too stunned to form words.

"John," he managed at last, unwilling to call the man "Dad," or "Father," or anything like that. "What are you doing here?"

The old man scowled and planted the cowboy hat back on his head. It was the same one Ty remembered from his youth, from those rare occasions his dad would make an appearance in his life.

"Helluva goddamn greeting for your old man," he muttered, pushing his way through the front door before Ty could object. He wore a dirty gray trench coat so tattered it was almost a cape. "I got your address from the county assessor," his father continued, looking around the room like a thief casing the joint.

Considering his last prison sentence was for burglary, that probably wasn't far from the truth.

The old man swiveled his gaze back to Ty. "Free internet at the library. You wouldn't believe the shit those county assessors put on the goddamn website. Addresses and how much people paid for their houses. It's all online if you know where to look for it." He cackled and tapped his forehead with one dirty fingernail. "You got your big brain from someplace, you know."

Ty said nothing. He was focused on figuring out how to get his father out of his home and out of his life before Ellie or Henry came in from the back porch.

"Aren't you supposed to be in prison?" Ty asked.

"Early parole." His father gave a smug nod. "Happens a lot for non-violent crimes."

"So I recall," Ty said, folding his arms over his chest as a sharp shard of rage lodged itself between his ribs. "Not that all those early releases seemed to free up your time to visit your children or get a job or send child support to—"

"Oh, come on!" The old man waved one gnarled hand like that was water under the bridge. Like years of neglect could be erased by a simple hand gesture. "You're not still sore about that, are you?"

Ty stared at his father. "Why are you here?"

"I've turned over a new leaf." The old man adjusted his hat. "And when I saw Anna's engagement in the paper, I thought maybe I'd get in touch. You know, make amends, meet her new man, maybe walk her down the aisle."

Fresh fury washed through Ty's body. His hands curled into fists, lodged against his crossed arms. "Stay away from Anna," he growled.

The old man snorted. "I can't even find her. Wily little bitc—little bit of a thing." He cleared his throat. "I been looking, though. Was hoping you'd help me get in touch."

Ty took a few deep breaths, struggling to gain his composure. To formulate a response that contained the least amount of profanity possible.

He was still thinking about it when he heard a voice

behind him.

"Mr. Ty? I can't find the bathroom, and I hafta go *really* bad."

. . .

Ellie dashed into the room and caught Henry by the arm, ready to steer him back down the hall. She saw from the rigid set of Ty's posture that the man standing in the living room was no salesman, and she sensed now wasn't the time for inquiries or introductions.

"Henry, remember what I said?" She stooped down to her son's level, trying to shield him from the surly stranger's stare. "Let's look together down this hall right over—"

"Well, *hello.*"

Ellie cringed, not sure how the man had managed to make a benign two-word greeting sound lecherous. She turned to see the stranger leering at her. His voice sounded like Ty's voice if it had been pushed through a rock crusher and spit out the other end, and something about his eyes was familiar.

"Aren't you a pretty little thing." The man touched the brim of a dirty cowboy hat and continued to stare.

Ellie straightened up, putting herself between the stranger and her son. The old man elbowed Ty in the ribs and gave an approving nod. "I'm Johnny," he said. "Like Johnny Cash, ya know?" He grinned like someone proud of his own joke then stuck his hand out to Ellie. "Johnny Hendrix," he said. "I'm Ty's dad."

Realization pinged through her as she shook the old man's hand and darted a glance at Ty. His expression was stony, and he stared at their linked hands like he wanted to sever them apart with a saw.

Behind her, Henry stepped forward. "Your dad is Gentleman Ghost?" He looked from Ty to Johnny, an expression of wonder on his small face.

Ty found his tongue at last. "Uh…Gentleman Ghost?" He shot a baffled look at Ellie, but it was Henry who answered.

"Gentleman Ghost," Henry repeated. "From *Batman: the Brave and the Bold*. He wears a big hat like that one, and a gray cape, and he's in 'Terror on Dinosaur Island,' and that one episode where—"

"Ha!" The old man hooted like that was the funniest thing he'd ever heard. "You heard the kid," he said, turning back to Ty. "I'm a real motherfuckin' gentleman. The Gentleman Ghost. I like that."

The words seemed to jolt Ty from whatever trance he'd been in. With steel in his jaw, he stepped between Ellie and his father and put a hand on Ellie's shoulder. "Let me show you the bathroom," he said, taking Henry's hand and hustling him down the hall so fast that Ellie almost had to jog to keep up.

Ty looked back over his shoulder and shot a glance at his father. It was a look that suggested he'd glue the old man's eyebrows to his knees if he touched one single thing in that living room.

Ellie moved behind him, wondering if there was any way to make this awkward reunion less uncomfortable. As they turned into the master bedroom, Ty led them to a small bathroom tucked into the far corner of the house. "You guys can use this one," he said. "It's—uh—farther away than the guest bath."

Ellie nodded and ushered Henry inside. "Thanks," she said to Ty, patting Henry on the shoulder. "You go ahead, baby," she said. "I'll wait right here."

Ty nodded, relieved. As Henry closed the door behind him, Ellie took a few steps away from it. Ty did the same, and Ellie lowered her voice to a whisper.

"Are you okay?"

Looking far from okay, Ty raked his hands through his

hair. "Yeah." He glanced toward the living room. "I need to get back out there. I don't trust him alone."

"I understand." Ellie hesitated. Not sure if it was her place to ask questions. "I heard you say 'Anna' when I came in. Is there a problem with your sister?"

Ty's jaw clenched as he nodded. "Yeah. I need to make sure he doesn't find her. I need to—" He glanced at the bathroom door, but Henry was still safely out of earshot. "I need to warn her that he's out."

"Out?"

"Of prison. Again."

She must have looked alarmed because Ty put a hand on her shoulder. "He's not dangerous. Not like that, anyway. It's mostly car theft and forgery. Things like that."

"Oh, that's all." Ellie nodded, understanding now why they probably wouldn't be inviting Ty's father to Christmas dinner. Her heart ached for Ty, and she wondered how to make this better. "Do you want to call her?"

"Yeah. I should actually call his parole officer, too."

"Want me to keep an eye on your dad so you can do that privately?"

He looked conflicted for a second. She wished she could reassure him that this would all be okay. That they'd deal with this together. That having a criminal for a father didn't change how she saw him.

"I'm not leaving you alone with him," Ty muttered.

"You said yourself he's not dangerous," she said. "And you'll be fifteen feet away, well within earshot."

Uncertainty played across his face. He glanced back at the bathroom door. "If I stand here and make the call, I can head off Henry. I'll be two minutes, three tops."

"Okay." Ellie nodded and started toward the door. "I'll babysit your father. If he starts to run out the door with any valuables, I'll scream bloody murder and call 911."

Ty's expression was so haunted that she wanted to turn back and comfort him.

"I'm kidding, Ty. It's okay. I've got this. Make your calls." She turned and marched down the hall, straightening her spine to show she wasn't one to be trifled with.

"Thanks for waiting, Mr. Hendrix," she said. The old man had seated himself on the sofa, and his gaze swept over Ellie's body as she marched into the room. She suppressed the urge to cringe. "While Ty gets my son situated, can I grab you something to drink?"

The old man frowned. "Getting your son situated," he muttered, his tone mocking. "Lemme guess—that's code for calling my fucking parole officer."

From the end of the hall, Ty's voice rumbled. "Do not swear in this house!" he shouted. "Especially not in front of Ellie or Henry."

Knowing Ty could hear every word of the conversation gave Ellie a renewed sense of safety. She took a deep breath and hoped like hell Ty's call went fast.

"So your name's Ellie," he said. "You're fu—you're hooking up with my son?"

Ellie bit her lip and decided not to dignify that with a response. Even so, part of her wanted to argue. Wanted to shout, "this is more than just a hookup!" because that was true now.

The thought calmed her down. "I know there's milk in the fridge," she said. "Or I can grab you some water."

"Can't I get a beer?"

"I—uh—I don't think there's any beer."

She had no idea, but offering alcohol to a criminal seemed like a bad idea.

She moved toward the refrigerator, keeping an eye on Johnny the whole time. As she opened the door, she heard the old man snort. "No beer," he muttered. "Bullshit. My boy's just like his old man—loves a good IPA. I taught him to open beer bottles myself when he was still in diapers."

Ellie nodded, pretty sure that sort of childhood memory was precisely why Ty was so upset by his father showing up. Had Ty managed to reach Anna? She located a can of Coke in the fridge and pulled it out.

Pushing the door shut with her hip, she popped the top on the soda then headed back to the living room. "Here you go," she said. "Let me know if I can grab you a glass."

"Hmph," the old man grunted as he took a noisy slurp. "So, what do you do, Ellie?"

She shot a nervous glance down the hall as she heard a toilet flush. Would Ty be able to stall Henry? "I'm in sales," Ellie said carefully. "How about you?"

The old man snorted again, a sound familiar enough that it took her a second to place it. *Ty.* He made that noise all the time when he scoffed at something.

"I take it he hasn't told you about me." John folded his arms over his chest and stared her down. "I was kind of a shit when he was growing up. Apparently, he's still sore about it."

Ellie gave a bland nod, not willing to betray anything Ty had told her about foster homes or the deadbeat dad who spent more time in prison than he did at Little League games. Coming face-to-face with that dad now made her grateful Henry's father wasn't this bad. Chuck might have little involvement in their son's life, but he wasn't a criminal. That was something.

"I'm aware of Ty's childhood," Ellie said mildly. "So, what brings you by for a visit?"

There was that snort again. "I'm not here for a fuckin' tea party, doll." He took a noisy slurp of soda then belched. "Just trying to track down my daughter. I saw she's marrying a lawyer."

Ah. Realization dawned. So that's what this was about.

He thought Anna had money. Or access to free legal help or something. Rage bloomed in Ellie's chest, and she fought the urge to tell him exactly where to shove his intentions.

"Weddings are nice," Ellie said, still trying to keep things light.

John eyed her again, and Ellie kept her spine straight, not willing to let him see she was nervous.

"You want a word of advice, sweet tits?"

Fury fizzed in Ellie's veins, but she ordered herself to stay calm. "Please don't call me that," she said evenly. "And no, I don't particularly want advice." She folded her arms over her chest and kept her breathing even. "I'm not inclined to take tips from anyone who uses the term 'sweet tits' to address a woman he's just met."

John snorted and took another slug of Coke. "Run fast from this one," he said. "Ty? He's all kinds of fucked up."

This time it was Ellie's turn to scoff. "If he were—which I certainly don't believe—don't you think his upbringing would have something to do with that?"

Something flashed in the old man's eyes. He stared at her through narrowed slits then stood up, slamming the soda can on the end table. She curled her hands into fists, ready to defend herself if it came to that. Being a single mom had spurred her to take at least a dozen self-defense classes over the years. If push came to shove, she could damn well stand her ground.

"That's enough!"

The boom of Ty's voice made them both turn. He was storming down the hall toward them, anger making sharp creases in his forehead. "John. Your parole officer is on his way here right now. Looks like you're not supposed to set foot outside Polk County."

John frowned and gave a snort of rage. "Fuck that shit."

Ellie spotted her son right behind Ty, and his eyes widened

at the curse. She hustled over, putting her hands on Henry's shoulders and her body between the angry stranger and her child.

Ty stepped forward, ready to face down his father. "That's it!" Ty snarled. "I told you not to curse in my house. You'll wait on the porch until your parole officer gets here."

Ellie felt Henry's shoulders stiffen beneath her palms. She watched as her little boy processed everything—the fact that Ty was angry, that John had said something inappropriate, that the moment called for a strong reaction.

"Yeah," Henry said, puffing out his chest and stepping up beside Ty. "Gentlemen don't talk like that," he said. "And you're a squirrel fucker!"

Ellie heard herself gasp, and she glanced at Ty in time to catch his reaction. Horror flashed quickly, but it was gone in an instant and replaced with something worse.

Embarrassment.

Guilt.

Defeat.

Johnny said nothing, seeming at a loss for words for the first time since he'd set foot in the house. Ellie kept her hands on Henry's shoulders, knowing there'd be time for a scolding later. Right now, Ty looked like a man who'd been punched in the gut.

When he turned to face her, his expression had gone blank.

"Wait here," he told her. "I'll be right back. My father will not."

Ellie nodded as Ty hauled his father up off the couch and marched him to the door. Something in Ty's posture, in the harsh set of his jaw, told her some line had just been crossed. That something had just split wide open inside him.

She shivered and bent down to hug her son.

# Chapter Sixteen

The police cruiser pulled away with Ty's father in the backseat. As the car turned the corner, the old man caught his eye and flipped him the bird.

"Fuck you, too, Johnny," Ty muttered under his breath.

Then he turned and stared at his own front door. In case he wasn't sure what had to be done, the words he'd just uttered had underscored it.

Who the hell was he kidding, thinking he could be any sort of role model for a child? That he'd ever be the sort of guy a woman like Ellie deserved? Breaking things off now would be the kindest thing to do. He needed to act now, before anyone got too attached.

*You're already attached.*

He shook his head and pushed open the door. His heart was heavy as he moved through the living room. Ellie and Henry sat on the couch, and they looked up as he walked in. Her blue eyes were bright with concern, and the compassion in her expression nearly stole his resolve.

But the memory of Henry cursing like a sailor put it all

right back.

Ty picked his keys up off the side table by the door. "It's getting late," he said. "I should probably run you guys home."

Ellie looked at him a moment, then nodded. She got to her feet, reaching down to offer a hand to Henry.

Henry's response wasn't nearly as stoic. "But you said you'd play soccer with me," he said. "And that we'd watch me on TV."

The words hit Ty like a hundred scalding pebbles hurled at his throat. The disappointment in the kid's eyes left his whole body aching. All the more reason he needed to end this. Now, before he caused more damage.

"It's getting dark, sweetie," Ellie pointed out as she handed Henry his glass of milk and signaled him to polish it off. "You wouldn't be able to see the ball."

She shot a look at Ty, probably waiting for him to back her up or to offer a makeup date for the soccer game or the video viewing.

But there'd be no makeup date. There'd be no more anything.

"Sorry, kiddo." Ty's throat tightened, and he ordered himself to look Henry in the eye. He owed the kid that much. "I wish it could be different."

God, that was the understatement of the year. Ty's chest ached, like a Clydesdale was standing on his ribs. He shifted his keys from one hand to the other as he studied Ellie, committing every detail to memory.

*You won't ever see her again. Not if you do what needs to be done.*

Ellie shoved her feet back into her flip-flops and looked at him. Her expression was curious, which made Ty's heart clench like a fist. She had to know something was up. Ty had never been good at hiding his feelings.

"Come on, baby." Ellie helped Henry get his sandals on,

then stood and smoothed the front of her T-shirt. When she met Ty's eyes again, he lost his breath.

*You okay?* she mouthed.

He nodded once then pushed open the front door. The air outside felt fifty degrees colder. A neighbor's black cat darted across the road, turning to shoot Ty a look of feline contempt.

*You're not the only one disgusted, cat.*

The drive home was tense, though as far as Ty could tell, Henry didn't seem to notice. The boy chattered the whole way, offering a running commentary about the Batman episode where Gentleman Ghost first matched wits against Batman.

"And see, Gorilla Grodd wants to turn all the humans into monkeys, but Batman and Plastic Man think that's stupid, so they get together and—"

Ellie put her hand on Ty's knee, and Ty flicked his gaze to her.

"You sure you're all right?" she whispered.

Ty hesitated then shook his head. He wished he could talk to her about it. Part of him wanted to tell her exactly what he was feeling. To explain why everything had come crashing down the second he'd seen his father in his living room. He wished there were some way for her to reassure him he'd rise above it. That maybe he'd learn to be a good guy, the sort of guy who wouldn't drag them both down to his level.

But that wasn't true at all.

The compassion in her eyes made him blurt out anyway, "Seeing my father again—"

He stopped, glancing at Henry in the backseat. The boy was still chattering, oblivious to the tension in the front seat.

"—So then Gentleman Ghost shows up with guns, and he's all, 'pew-pew-pew.'"

Henry kept going, fingers pointed like pistols, delighted just to be telling his story.

"I get it," Ellie whispered beside him. "I've been thinking

about that a lot, actually."

Confused, Ty hit his blinker and merged onto the highway toward Ellie's place. "About Gentleman Ghost?"

"No." Ellie shook her head then glanced over her shoulder at Henry. The boy was still talking, showing no interest in the adult conversation happening two feet away.

"And then Plastic Man, he makes his hands into big fists, like this—see? So Batman is all, 'You stop that right now, Gorilla Grodd!' And then Gorilla Grodd says—"

"I've been thinking about fathers," Ellie whispered, so softly it took Ty a few seconds to be sure he'd heard her right. "About how a lousy one is so much worse for a kid than no father at all."

Ty felt Plastic Man's fist slam hard into his gut. Ellie's words took the breath out of him, made him absolutely sure of what he had to do. As he took the exit toward her house, she put a hand on his knee. "Would you mind dropping Henry at Jason and Miriam's place?"

"Sure," he said.

"Thanks. They texted while you were outside with your dad. They wanted to have him over for a Popsicle and hear all about the trip before bedtime."

*Popsicles.*

The summer before his grandmother passed, she'd comforted him with a grape Popsicle every time his father failed to show for a scheduled visit. By the end of August, Ty's mouth was stained purple and his eyes were bloodshot from crying.

*Jesus.*

He clenched the steering wheel harder.

"No problem." Ty turned onto their shared street, grateful he'd have a few moments alone with Ellie. It would be easier that way.

The second he pulled up in front of Jason and Miriam's

place, Ellie hopped out. "I'll be two seconds," she said. "Come on, baby."

"Wait," Henry said. "I hafta say good night to Mr. Ty, right? I'm not gonna see him again."

"Not tonight," Ellie agreed, and Ty's chest ached again. The seat belt felt too tight around it, so he unfastened the latch and got out of the car. Henry was already out of his seat, standing in the grass median beside the mailbox. He put a hand up, and Ty stooped down to hug him before realizing the kid just wanted a handshake.

*You can't even get that right*, he told himself, hugging the kid tighter.

"Good night, kiddo," he said. "Be good for your aunt and uncle."

"Okay." Henry pulled back and grinned up at him, eyes bright behind his smudged glasses. "And maybe tomorrow we can play soccer."

A slick spear of ice slid between Ty's ribs, and he lost his breath. "Maybe."

With that, Ty added lying to a child to his list of crimes.

Ellie didn't say much as they drove the few hundred feet to her front door. She kept glancing at him sideways, waiting for Ty to make the first move. He gathered their bags out of the trunk and followed her up the walk, trudging like a man headed to the execution chamber.

The second the door closed behind him, Ellie turned to face him. "I know you're upset about your dad showing up like that," she said. "Obviously it wasn't ideal, but I want you to know I'm not offended or upset about—"

"We need to break up."

Ellie's eyes flashed with surprise. The bags slid from Ty's grip, making a dull thud in her entryway. He raked one hand through his hair, knowing he needed to rip the Band-Aid off quickly.

"I know we barely got started," he said, struggling to explain. "But that's why I think it's important to end things fast. Before anyone gets too attached."

"Before anyone gets too attached." She stared at him, a mystified look on her face. "You think I'm not attached?"

"I know *I'm* attached," he said. "That's the problem, Ellie. I care too much about you and Henry to ruin your lives."

She blinked hard, and Ty wondered if she was struggling to hold back tears. His throat was thick and tight, and he wasn't sure how to fight back his own flood of emotion.

"I don't understand," she said. "How would you be ruining our lives?"

Ty clawed at his hair again, knowing this wouldn't make sense to her. But he owed her an explanation, no matter how shitty it might be. "I grew up with the world's worst father, Ellie. The rare times he came sweeping into my life, the only things he left behind were disappointment and bad habits."

"I don't see what that has to do with—"

"Tonight, Ellie…it was so clear. That's exactly what I'm bringing into your life. Into Henry's life. Bad habits and regrets and the certainty that this whole thing will eventually blow up and leave an innocent kid sobbing into his pillow."

"You don't think Henry will miss you if you walk away now?"

He shook his head, regretting the small ripples of sadness that might trickle through the boy's life over the next day or two. But how much harder would it be six months from now? Six years?

"It would be worse later. Trust me. Once he started counting on me. Or you did. Don't you see?"

She stared at him a long moment, and Ty's head throbbed. He wanted to take back every word he'd just said. To tell her he didn't mean it, that he really did want to be with her.

*That'll only make it harder,* he reminded himself. *When*

*this ends—and you know it'll end—it'll just be tougher then.*

Ty took a shaky breath. His heart was a cold, dead lump in the middle of his chest. "Before he met me, how many times, exactly, had Henry used the phrase, 'squirrel fucker?'"

Ellie shook her head and wiped the edge of one eye with the heel of her hand. But in that instant, there was a flicker of uncertainty—of the knowledge that he might be right.

"That's not a fair question," Ellie said.

"You know what else isn't fair?" Ty took a shaky breath, trying to control his voice. The scent of cookies and fabric softener hung in the air of Ellie's apartment, choking him with memories of home and happiness. Things he'd never had. "It's not fair for me to get Henry's hopes up about a paycheck, then having him find out there *is* no paycheck. Or playing soccer. Or watching a video. Do you know what it does to a kid to find out over and over again that a grown-up he trusted flat-out *lied* to him?"

Ellie shook her head, eyes brimming with tears. "Ty, you can't possibly be comparing a childhood of neglect and emotional abuse with a few minor incidents of disappointment and foul language," she said. "If there were any comparison at all, half the parents in America would have Children's Services knocking at their door."

"That's just it, Ellie." It was almost like someone skewered his spleen with a steak knife, and he wished more than anything for a way to undo this—tonight's regrettable incidents, his whole childhood, all of it. "I'm not a parent," he said. "I'm not cut out to be a father or a husband or a boyfriend or even a role model. Those options aren't on the table for me. Growing up the way I did—there's no way I can possibly bring anything but heartache and frustration to your life."

Ellie stared at him. "And you don't think I can judge that for myself?"

"No," he said. "You don't know me. Not like you think you do."

She flinched at that, and Ty wanted to take back the words. But they were true, and she needed to know it. "Ellie, the real me isn't a good guy," he said. "He's the kind of guy who doesn't step in to film your son's school event in a pinch. He's the kind of guy who leaves you alone in his living room with a convicted felon."

There was that flicker of uncertainty again. The look in her eyes that said she recognized there might be something to his warning. That maybe this was for the best.

She stared at him for a long time. There was sadness in her eyes, but something else, too. Understanding, maybe. The knowledge that he was right. That she was better off without him.

She had to know that, right?

"I thought you were different," she murmured. "I didn't think you were the kind of guy who'd cut and run at the first sign of trouble."

The words hung there between them, unspoken. *The kind of guy like Henry's father. Like Ty's own father.*

"I am," he said in a voice halfway between a sob and a growl. "I'm exactly that kind of guy."

Ellie shook her head as tears spilled down her cheeks. But she didn't sob. She didn't break down. God, even now she was the strongest woman he'd ever known.

She stared at him, digesting his words as her blue eyes shimmered. Her hands clenched, white-knuckled, at her sides, and he almost wished she'd punch him. God knew he deserved to hurt.

Which stung worse? The look in her eyes that said she didn't believe him?

Or the one that said deep down she knew he was right.

"I think you're making a mistake, Ty."

Her voice was soft. Almost as soft as her skin, which he'd never touch again. He hated that thought. Maybe more than he hated himself.

He swallowed hard, wishing he could reach for her. Wishing for so many other things he'd never have.

"Maybe I am making a mistake," he said. "But I'm keeping you from making a bigger one."

And with that, he turned and walked out the door.

• • •

"Of all the bullshit reasons for a breakup!" Across the table, Miriam stabbed a hunk of chicken breast with her fork and glared.

Ellie sighed. "He does have a point. My job is to protect Henry, and if Ty himself thinks he's a bad influence—" She stopped there, not willing to finish the sentence. Staring down at her salad, she wondered when saying his name would stop feeling like someone had shoved her heart into a bench vice and started cracking the handle.

She was having lunch with Jason and Miriam at a café next to the community pool where Henry took swimming lessons. Parents had been kicked out after a crowd of camera-wielding helicopter moms fell into the pool, so Miriam, Jason, and Ellie had retreated to the café next door for lunch.

Her brother watched her. He sat stoic and silent beside his fuming wife, thankfully not pulling the overprotective big brother act he'd employed when Chuck left.

Unsatisfied by her husband's lack of fury, Miriam jabbed an elbow into Jason's ribs. "Don't you have anything to say?" she asked.

Jason frowned. "Asshole," he offered helpfully, then picked up his ice water and took a swig.

Miriam turned back to Ellie. "I love Ty, don't get me

wrong," she said. "But what the fucking hell is wrong with him?"

"Well, for starters," Ellie said, "He was concerned about the effect it might have on Henry to be around an adult who uses profanity."

Jason and Miriam looked at each other then burst out laughing.

"I'm sorry, we shouldn't find that funny." Miriam stabbed her salad again, one hand resting on her belly. The baby kicked in response, making her whole belly ripple as Miriam chewed another bite of chicken. "It's just that if cursing's what separates the bad parents from the good ones, we're all pretty much doomed."

Ellie sighed. "But you don't curse around Henry." She glanced at her brother. "Much," she amended, remembering the time he'd whacked himself with a hammer helping Henry hang a Seattle Mariners poster on his wall.

Jason gave her a small smile and reached across the table to offer a brotherly hand-squeeze. "Sorry, El," he said. "I'm sorry you have to go through this again."

Ellie's throat ached, and she had to look away. She couldn't face the sympathy in his eyes, or the fact that she'd gone and fallen for a guy who'd done the same thing her stupid ex had.

Dammit, anyway.

Miriam stabbed a crouton. "Honey, you know as well as I do that it's not about the cursing," Miriam said. "It's about Ty's abandonment issues. It's him thinking he has no choice but to become his father. Maybe it's a guy thing."

Ellie looked up to see her brother nodding and regarding his wife with a thoughtful expression. "She has a point," he said, turning back to Ellie. "Remember how Dad was always telling me to watch out for you? 'It's your job to protect your sister,' he'd say."

Jason's impression of their father's growly baritone

made tears prick the back of Ellie's eyelids. She nodded. "I remember. I thought he meant sticking up for me on the playground when bullies pulled my pigtails."

"He meant that, too."

She looked at her brother, seeing something in his eyes she hadn't noticed before. Ellie licked her lips. "But also that it was your job to raise me after they died?"

Jason shook his head. "I didn't do it out of obligation," he said. "I did it because I love you, dumbass."

"I love you, too, dumbass." The tears were welling thicker now, and she stopped to dab the corner of one eye with a napkin.

"My point is that a guy can't help but internalize stuff like that," Jason said. "The things his dad says to him, the sort of example the old man sets—we soak that shit up like little sponges."

Beside him, Miriam nodded. "Poor Ty believed he'd never become anything other than a shit-soaked sponge." She frowned at her salad, then stabbed another bite.

"You know, it's actually a good thing he wants to break things off," Jason said.

Both women glared at him, and Ellie felt Miriam kick Jason under the table.

"Too soon, hon," Miriam said.

"That's not what I meant," he said. "I mean it's a sign that his first instinct is to protect you. He feels guilty about not being a good enough father figure."

"You're suggesting guilt is the sign of a good dad?" Ellie thought about that a minute, twirling her fork through a pile of kale salad. "I'm not sure Chuck feels too guilty about short-changing Henry on child support."

"Exactly!" Jason nodded and polished off the last of his salmon.

"I think you just hit the nail on the head," Miriam said.

"What separates the good guys from the shitty ones is whether they even notice when they screw up. Whether it bothers them when that happens. Because let's face it—they're all going to screw up."

"All of us," Jason agreed cheerfully, swiping at his beard with a napkin. "How's Henry handling things, anyway?"

"You mean with Ty not being around?" She shrugged. "He's asked about him a couple of times in the last week. I guess it's a good thing it was still so new. Henry only knew him as someone I worked with, so he's not reading too much into it."

"Ty was good with Henry," Miriam said. "Regardless of what the dumbshit thinks, I have eyes. I saw them at that ball game together. Ty might not have had a lot of finesse, but he was kind and genuine. Kids pick up on that."

"For sure." Ellie took a sip of tea, wishing her heart didn't ache with the memory of Ty and Henry together. "Speaking of Henry, did I tell you what he did?"

"Brought a vibrator to show-and-tell?" Jason suggested, earning a swat from Miriam.

"Of course not," Miriam said. "You know she keeps that stuff under lock and key."

"I know," Jason said. "And I've been trying to find the key."

Ellie rolled her eyes and picked up her fork again. "Henry signed me up to speak during career week," she said. "I had no idea he'd done it until his teacher left a voicemail this morning trying to nail down a date."

"Yikes," Jason said. "Is she expecting you to give a demo of the different kinds of lube?"

Ellie shook her head. "She has no idea what I do for a living. All she knows is that I'm in sales. I haven't had the heart to call back and explain things."

"Yeah, that seems like it would be better as an in-person

conversation," Miriam agreed. "Plus, you can offer her a free Happy Jammer couple's vibe so she'll be more understanding."

Ellie gave a dry laugh. "That's exactly what I need. A reputation as the mom who gives sex toys to her son's teacher."

"What are you going to do?" Jason asked.

Ellie shrugged and swirled her fork through a puddle of dressing. "Mrs. Colt asked me to meet with her Tuesday morning before class starts," she said. "I'll explain things then, I guess."

Miriam nodded and dabbed her mouth with a napkin. The baby kicked again, jolting her whole body this time. She looked up at Ellie, eyes wide with excitement. "Did you see that?"

"I did," Ellie said, remembering what it was like when she was eight months pregnant with Henry. Back then, Chuck had cupped her belly in his hands and given Henry a pep talk about not hitting and kicking.

Her throat tightened. Chuck might be an asshole for leaving her. He might be an even bigger asshole for trying to get out of paying child support.

But as Jason rubbed Miriam's belly, cooing softly to the baby inside, it occurred to Ellie that she owed it to herself and to Henry to grab the asshole by the balls.

She threw down her napkin and glanced at her watch. "Do you guys mind hanging out here for just a second?"

Miriam looked up, her expression curious. "What's up?"

"I need to make a phone call."

Jason nodded then went back to rubbing Miriam's belly. "No problem, El," he said. "No matter what, we've got your back."

"Thank you," she said, hopeful for the first time all week. "I know you do."

• • •

Ellie glanced at her watch as she stepped into the quiet hallway outside the café restroom. She pulled out her phone, grateful she had another thirty minutes until Henry finished swimming lessons. This wouldn't take long, and even if it did, Jason and Miriam would look after her son.

Knowing that—and realizing that no matter what, she was a strong, single mom who could protect her own kid—gave her the strength to hit the speed-dial number she hadn't called for almost a year.

"Hello?"

"Chuck," she said, a little surprised he'd answered.

"Ellie." He sounded as surprised as she did.

She cleared her throat and pressed her back against the wall, steeling herself for the conversation. "I've gotten your letters," she said. "And the texts. And I had my lawyer look over everything."

"El," he said in that vaguely patronizing tone she'd always hated. "What's with the lawyer? We agreed when we split up that we'd handle it ourselves. That we didn't need the courts telling us what to do."

"Actually, no." Ellie tucked a strand of hair behind one ear as she struggled to keep her voice calm. "We didn't agree to that at all. That was your idea. Just like abandoning your wife and son was your idea. Just like failing to provide for his basic needs was your idea."

There was a long pause, followed by a sigh. "Ellie, be reasonable. I shouldn't have to stay in a job I hate just to support my kid."

"You know, that's where you're wrong." Ellie's fist clenched at her side, and she reminded herself it would hurt like hell to punch the wall. "That's *exactly* what you should do. That's exactly what a father does. Or you should find a new job while you continue chipping in for your son's medical bills."

"Money isn't everything," he said in a patronizing tone that made her want to rip his hair out.

"It's not, you're right," she said through gritted teeth. "But it sure comes in handy for school lunches and dentist visits and shoes to replace the ones he's outgrown."

"Ellie—"

"And in case you're forgetting, you're the one who pushed to have a child in the first place."

"I'm not forgetting." His voice was filled with irritation, and Ellie guessed he maybe had forgotten. "It's just—look, what the state calculates I'm supposed to pay is nuts. It's way too high."

"It's actually the bare minimum," she pointed out. "It's what the state has determined a living, breathing, gainfully employed father should contribute toward feeding and clothing and housing a child he chose to bring into the world."

"Right, but I hardly ever see him," he said. "I just think—"

"Whose fault is that?" Ellie interrupted as fire flared in her belly. "Who chose that, Chuck? Certainly not Henry."

Her ex sighed again. "You know my schedule is crazy."

"What I *know* is that our son is the number one priority. Always. That's what you signed on for the day you tossed my birth control pills in the trash and said, 'let's make a baby.'"

"Ellie—"

"What I *know* is that being a dad requires more than sperm donation," she interrupted, tired of him not getting it. "If you don't want to show up and take him to ball games or teach him to bodysurf, that's fine." Her heart twisted a little as she remembered Ty doing those things. As she pictured Henry's grin when Ty showed him how to make a lion face.

But this wasn't about Ty. This was about Henry, and about Ellie knowing how to stand on her own two feet.

And right now, she wanted to plant one of them in her ex-husband's ass.

"Look, I'm more than capable of molding our son into a decent man on my own," she said. "And I'm also not going to be the one to tell him his father's a raging asshole. But I want you to think long and hard about how you want your son to regard you twenty years from now. Will he remember you as they guy who forgot birthday cards and couldn't be bothered to call him at Christmas? Or will he remember you as a guy who made an effort—even a tiny one—to make sure he was okay?"

She let the words hang there for a moment, giving him time to consider. To make the right decision. "Which will it be, Chuck?"

On the other end of the line, her ex was silent. When he cleared his throat, Ellie braced herself to do battle again.

"Wow," he said. "I didn't know it meant that much to you."

"Damn right, it does."

"Okay, then. I…uh…I'll crunch some numbers. And, um—would it be okay if I called Henry on Sunday just to say hi?"

"You can call him anytime," she said. "You know that. All I want is for him to know he's loved. That even if you're not perfect, you give a shit about him. That's what matters."

"Damn," he said. "What's gotten into you?"

Ellie took a calming breath, surprised to see her hands weren't shaking. That she felt relief instead of anger. "I'm standing up for my kid, Chuck. This is about me. And him. And making sure he has the sort of A-plus parenting he deserves."

And with that, she hung up on her ex-husband.

# Chapter Seventeen

Ty turned away from the computer monitor and looked up at his sister. "What do you think?"

Anna's eyes glittered with tears. She wore a bright pink sweater and a polka-dotted scarf that she used to dab the corner of one eye as she slid off her chair.

"It's amazing," she said, leaning down to hug him before Ty made it to his feet for a proper embrace. "I never knew my big brother was so talented."

Ty patted her back, awkward and out-of-sorts. Their late-in-life connection meant he and Anna were still pretty new to displays of affection, and it felt odd to be sitting in his office after work accepting hearty praise and hugs from his half-sister.

Odd, but *nice*. Since he hadn't slept well all week, Ty would take all the nice that was offered to him.

"I'm glad you like it," he said as Anna let go and slid back onto her seat. "Can't say I've ever done a digital wedding invitation before, but I think it turned out pretty well."

"It's wonderful," she said, tucking a dark strand of

hair behind one ear. "Thanks for working around my crazy schedule, too. You're sure it's okay to do this in your office?"

"Positive," Ty said. "One of the upsides of being a partner."

"I'm proud of you, big brother. You've come a long way."

"We both have."

She squeezed his hand, and something pinched tight in the center of his chest. Human contact was nice, even if it was his sister.

Ellie had emailed yesterday with a breezy note about finding a different space to rent for her after-hours parties. *"Thanks for everything!"* she'd signed off at the end, the finality of it making Ty ache all over.

"Seriously, Ty." Anna took a sip of the kombucha he'd handed her, which made his throat squeeze the way it did every time he heard Ellie's voice in those damn commercials. "Thanks for doing this. I can't ever repay you."

"Sure you can," he said. "Save a dance for me at the wedding."

"That I can do," she said.

Ty leaned back in his chair grateful for his sister's company. "Martin is a great guy."

"I know. I'm lucky to be marrying him."

"He's the lucky one." He hesitated, not sure it was his place to ask the question that was on his mind. "You think you'll have kids?"

"Definitely! Actually, we've already been trying—"

"Aaaah!" Ty held up his hands and pretended to cover his ears. "I don't need details."

She laughed and gave him a swat. "You'll be a great uncle."

Ty winced but tried to hide it. He couldn't think of anything to say, so he turned back to his monitor and made a quick adjustment to the sound on the video.

"I keep meaning to thank you for the other thing you

did." Anna's voice was softer now, and Ty could guess what she meant.

"The engagement photos?" He toggled to Photoshop and pulled up the series of images, unexpectedly uncomfortable with the change in conversation. "I'm not really a still photographer, but I think they turned out pretty nice. If you want, I'd be happy to—"

"I was talking about Dad," Anna said. "About heading him off so he wouldn't show up on my doorstep."

"Right." Ty nodded, not sure what else to say.

"You have great instincts," she said. "I probably would have let him waltz right back through the door and into my life. Hell, I would have invited the asshole to the wedding."

"There was no way for you to know he planned to shake down your new husband for half-a-million bucks."

"No, but you did. Well, not the specifics, but you were guarded enough to be suspicious."

"Yeah," Ty agreed, not sure that was necessarily a trait worth bragging about. "I just know you don't deserve that sort of crap in your life."

He looked back in time to see her smiling, her face bright and open and grateful. "Well," she said, "I don't know what I did to deserve you, but it must have been pretty good."

Ty offered a hollow smile in return, not feeling much like the good guy. He cleared his throat, eager to change the subject. "I can do a little more editing on this last series of imaging. If we wanted it to be perfect, I'd just need to—"

"I don't want it to be perfect," she interrupted. "That's not what marriage is about. A few flaws give it character."

"Character," Ty repeated, not sure he understood. But she was the one getting married, not him. Clearly, she'd figured out something he hadn't.

"So, you're okay with next Tuesday for the tux fitting?" Anna asked.

"I can make that work."

Anna stood up, beaming, then bent to kiss him on the forehead. "Thanks again, Ty. For everything."

"My pleasure. Want me to send you a link for the video and the photos?"

"That would be great. Actually, will you copy Martin, too? Let me give you his address."

Anna reached across him to grab a sticky-note pad then bent low to scrawl the email. Ty tried to scoot back but hit the corner of his desk, so he was stuck with his sister leaning awkwardly over his lap.

Naturally, that's when Miriam walked in. She froze in the doorway, eyes wide with surprise. As she started to back up, Ty held up a hand.

"Miriam, this is my sister, Anna," he said. "Anna, this is the boss lady, Miriam. She owns the company."

"Oh!" Anna stood up and hurried across the room, hand extended in greeting. "It's so great to finally meet you. I've heard so much about you."

"Likewise," Miriam said, even though Ty was pretty sure he'd never said Anna's name to her. Being tight-lipped about his family had its downsides. "It's a pleasure to meet you. Sorry, I didn't mean to interrupt. I can come back another time."

"No, it's fine," Anna said. "I was just leaving. Great meeting you!"

She stooped down to give Ty one last hug then scurried out of the room. Miriam watched her go then turned back to face Ty. "I hope I didn't chase her off."

"Nah, she really was leaving. She just stopped by to see the engagement video I made for her."

"I'd love to see it sometime," she said, easing onto the barstool Anna had just vacated. "But first, I have some good news."

Relief sloshed in Ty's veins. Miriam had been nothing but professional since his split with Ellie, but he'd sensed a prickliness just the same. It wasn't anger or wrath or anything like that. Just a hint of disappointment mixed with the occasional look that said, *man, you messed up.*

Or maybe Ty was projecting.

"What's the news?" he asked.

"I had lunch today with Bob Weisinger. The marketing director for Great Wolf Lodge?"

"Oh yeah?" Ty gestured at his phone. "I had a voicemail from him an hour ago, but it was too late to call him back by the time I got it."

"He was calling to tell you that you won the RFP," she said. "We got the job!"

She held up her hand for a high-five, and Ty gave her palm an obedient slap. The gesture reminded him of his last high-five with Henry and the fact that he hadn't seen the kid for over a week.

It made him a lot sadder than he thought it would.

"That's great," Ty said. "Congratulations!"

"Why the hell are you congratulating me? You're the one who landed the job. This is your first big win since we launched Speak Up."

"You're right," Ty said, annoyed to realize he felt hollow. It was his video with Henry and Ellie that had clinched the deal, and he knew it.

"He loved your video," Miriam said, reading his mind. "He kept talking about how it wasn't just a bunch of pretty images. That you showed a connection to the subject. That you brought the viewer into that connection and made it real."

A hot ball of lead wedged itself in Ty's throat, making it hard for him to breathe. He tried anyway, taking a few gulps of air and hoping Miriam didn't notice.

No such luck. She stared at him a moment then folded

her hands over her bulging baby belly. "Do you mind if I speak frankly for a second?"

"Go right ahead." Like she'd ever needed permission.

Miriam took a deep breath. "What in fucking hell is wrong with you?"

Ty flinched, feeling his throat pinch around the lead ball. "What do you mean?"

"Spare me, Ty. We've worked together for more than six years. Let's be honest."

"Okay." He folded his hands on his desk and tried to look professional. "I care about Ellie and Henry a lot. I want what's best for them, and you do, too."

Miriam shook her head a little sadly. "It sounds like a bullshit line, but I can tell you mean it," she said. "That's the really depressing thing."

"Miriam, with all due respect, you don't know me that well. I know how much it sucks to get attached and then lose someone," he said softly. "And I know it's easier to cut things off before that can happen."

She didn't respond, so Ty looked up to see her studying him with something that looked like pity. "I think you underestimated Ellie's feelings for you," she said. "And I think you *really* underestimated yours for her."

"Maybe." He took a shaky breath, not sure how much he should share. Did it matter at this point? "You don't know the backstory here. You don't know about my childhood and the sort of shitty personality traits it left me with."

"You ever read romance novels, Ty?"

That threw him for a loop. "What?"

"Romance novels," she said, unclasping her hands from around her belly. "I love them. I've read some amazing ones over the last years, and a few shitty ones, too. Want to know what the shitty ones have in common?"

Ty shook his head, not sure where she was going with this

but relieved it seemed to have taken her off the subject of Ellie and Henry for the moment.

"I have no idea," he said.

"Backstory," Miriam said. "In bad romance novels, it's like the author feels the need to fill those first few chapters with every last detail of a character's history. Who his parents were or how she liked her first job or whether the hero's brother stole his girlfriend in high school. But the thing is, none of that matters."

"I'm not so sure about that," Ty said, a little perplexed to realize he was arguing about romance novels when he'd never read one. "Someone's history matters a lot when it comes to making them who they are."

"Exactly," Miriam said. "And you can see who they *are* by how they act now. That's what matters."

Ty frowned, not sure he was picking up on the metaphor. But maybe he should stop dancing around it. Maybe she didn't know how badly he'd screwed up.

"I taught her kid to swear," Ty said. "And I bummed him out over and over by promising shit I couldn't deliver."

Miriam shook her head, not doing a very good job of hiding her, 'man, you're a dumbass' look. "You don't get credit for the swearing," she said. "You might have taught him some more creative forms, but Jason's been cursing around the kid since he was in utero."

Ty sighed, appreciating her attempt at placating him, even if he didn't buy it. "He's better off without someone like me in his life. They both are."

"You're joking, right?" Miriam rolled her eyes. "You took her kid to a ballgame and taught him to bodysurf at a water park," Miriam countered. "And you did double-duty by making his mother come her brains out." She put a hand up, heading Ty off before he said anything in response. "Don't worry, she didn't kiss and tell. I'm just guessing, based on the glow she had every time you two had time alone."

Ty frowned and fiddled with his mouse. "I'm not sure I should be talking about this with my boss."

"For the last time, Ty—I'm not your goddamn boss. You're a partner in this firm now, and the director of Speak Up."

He quirked an eyebrow at her. "So, does that mean I can ask you to leave?"

"No, because I still own the building."

"Fair enough." Ty sighed, but he wasn't disappointed. Truth be told, he didn't want her to go away. Since he'd broken things off with Ellie, he hadn't talked with anyone about this. It was nice to share with Miriam, even if he did still think of her as the boss.

"I miss her," he admitted. "And Henry. I miss them a lot."

"They miss you, too."

Something flared in his chest, but he refused to believe it was hope. It was too late for that, wasn't it?

"Can I tell you a secret, Ty?"

He looked at her and nodded. "Of course."

"When Jason and I started dating, I felt like an idiot with Henry. I'd never been around kids before, so the idea of getting involved with a guy who was like a surrogate dad to his nephew scared the shit out of me."

"So how did you handle it?" His eagerness belied the cool-guy tone he'd been trying for, but Miriam didn't comment.

"I did it anyway," she said. "Even though I was scared. Even though I knew I was going to screw it up. I figured if I kept doing it, I'd eventually screw up less."

"But how did you know you weren't screwing up Henry?"

"Because I kept showing up," she said. "And he kept smiling. You can tell a lot from that."

Ty sat quietly, digesting that. He didn't say anything for a long time, not until Miriam leaned across his lap to grab his computer mouse. "Let me show you something," she said.

"Ugh," said Ty, reeling from the heft of her mighty baby-belly pressing into his arm. "How about if you tell you what you're looking for and I can pull it up on the—"

"There!" Miriam sat back, triumphant, and pointed at the screen. "Remember that first shoot you did with Ellie? The one where she was nervous as hell and you tried to put her at ease?"

It seemed like so long ago. "Vaguely," he said. What he did remember was the smell of Ellie's hair and the warmth of her breast grazing the heel of his hand.

"Did you know the camera was rolling when you came out from behind it to talk to her?"

Ty frowned, trying to recall the details of that afternoon. "I haven't seen it," he said. "I just put it out on the server so you could check it out if you wanted."

Miriam jabbed one manicured nail at the screen. "Watch it now. Notice the way you both light up when you're talking to each other. If you can do that and then come back and tell me you don't belong together, I'll shut up about this forever."

She smiled then heaved herself up out of the chair. Ty reached out to steady her, but she waved him off. "I'm good," she said. "Just a couple more weeks to go."

Headed toward the door, she turned and pointed at him. "Be good to yourself, Ty. You deserve it, too."

He stared at her for a long time then nodded. "Thanks."

As she vanished through the door, Ty turned back to his computer monitor. He looked at the file she'd cued up, hesitating. Editing the footage from Great Wolf Lodge had hurt like hell, but this was different. This was Ellie alone. Ellie and him together Could he really do this?

*Don't be a chickenshit.* He clicked the file.

Ellie's face appeared on the monitor, nervous and flushed as she sat there alone in her pale blue dress. There was fear in her eyes, but also determination. The simple loveliness of her face hit Ty like a fist to the sternum.

*"I'm sorry,"* she said to the camera. *"I feel dumb."*

Wow. Had it really been only a few weeks since she'd been terrified of the camera? He watched, spellbound, as she bit her lip and stole a nervous glance at the light.

*"How about we try this."* It was his own voice this time as he slid into the frame. *"I'm just going to sit right here, and we're going to chat like normal people."*

But there was more to this conversation than a simple chat. It was there in the way they leaned close like two people sharing the warmth of a campfire. It was there in Ellie's eyes as they sparked with interest at his story about the asshole Navy admiral. It was there in the way he watched the side of her face as she turned to grab her water glass, his expression so full of love and admiration and hope that he looked like a whole different person.

Something magical had happened that afternoon. Had Ellie known?

He sure as hell hadn't. How had he missed it?

*"That's so sweet,"* Ellie said on camera. Her gaze was fixed on him, and the way she smiled brought back a clearer memory of that conversation—how her voice had stirred something inside him, like two puzzle pieces finally clicking together.

How had he been so blind?

*"I believe in karma."* It was his own voice speaking this time, and the look on his face answered his question. He had known. Deep down, he'd known from the start that Ellie meant something to him.

*"If you take the chance to be a jerk to someone, someone's bound to do the same to you,"* he continued, his gaze fixed on Ellie's face. *"Stop the flow of assholery and respond with kindness instead, and you'll eventually get the same in return."*

She lifted a hand to tuck a strand of hair behind one ear,

and his breath caught in his throat. Ty forced his lungs to take in air. Had anyone ever looked at him that way, ever?

Not in his whole life. Not ever.

But it wasn't just the way Ellie looked at him.

He stared at his own face, noticing the easing of lines he'd thought were permanently etched in his forehead. As the images flickered on his screen, his face came alive, and Ellie responded in turn.

*Jesus.*

The video was still playing as he reached for the phone. He hit the speed dial for Miriam, speaking before she had a chance to say hello.

"Do you honestly think there's a chance?"

Miriam laughed. She was too polite to say I-told-you-so, but he heard it anyway. "That was fast," she said. "I barely made it out of the parking lot. You're on speakerphone, by the way."

"Hi, Ty." Jason's voice. Ellie's brother.

The hell with it. Ty swallowed hard. Might as well get this over with.

"I know I don't deserve it, but I want another chance," he said. "Do you think there's any way she'd ever forgive me?"

"That depends," Miriam said. "Are you going to freak out on her again?"

"No," he said. "I mean, I'll do my best not to."

"And do you genuinely care about her?" Jason asked. "Her and Henry, I mean."

"I love her, okay?" he said. The words stunned him as they tumbled out of his mouth, but the second he said them, he knew it was true. "I'm in love with Ellie. I need to find a way to tell her. No," he said, stopping himself. "To *show* her. I need to find a way to show her. Can you help?"

Miriam laughed again, but Ty didn't take it personally. The laughter sounded joyful, and Ty needed more of that in his life right now.

"You're going to have to figure this out for yourself, Ty," Miriam said. "The relationship stuff, I mean. It's something everyone has to learn the hard way."

"I know, I know," he said, impatient for advice and eager to win Ellie back. "And I have a few thoughts about convincing her to give me another shot, but I need some help."

"Good," Miriam said. "I have an idea, too."

# Chapter Eighteen

As Ellie eased her station wagon into a parking space at the elementary school, she glanced in the rearview mirror at Henry.

He met her eye and beamed at her. "Are you coming to school with me?"

The excitement in Henry's voice was contagious, and Ellie caught herself smiling. "Just for a few minutes," she said. "Your teacher wanted to talk with me this morning, remember?"

"Uh-huh." Henry frowned. "Are you in trouble, Mommy?"

Ellie shook her head, not sure whether to laugh or wince. "No, I just need to visit with Mrs. Colt," she said. "Come on. I'll walk with you to class."

"Yeah!" He unbuckled his seat belt and scurried out of his booster, snatching his little Batman backpack before Ellie had even closed her car door.

"Whoa," Ellie said as she grabbed his hand. "A little eager to get to class today?"

"Uh-huh." He towed her along, hustling as they made

their way to the front doors. "It's career week, and everyone's been bringing famous people. Toby brought his big brother who's a dump truck driver, and Emma's mom came yesterday to tell us about cutting up brains."

"That does sound impressive," Ellie said, crossing her fingers Emma's mother was a surgeon and not a serial killer.

"Yeah," Henry said. "But my mom's the coolest." He grinned up at her, swinging her hand as she walked. "I told Hank and Sadie and Peter and—well, everyone that you're gonna talk, too."

"Right," Ellie said, her twinges of guilt reminding her of Ty. "About that," she continued, pushing aside the ache that stirred every time she remembered he wasn't in her life anymore. "I'm so flattered that you want me to talk to your class, sweetie. It means a lot to me that you're proud of me like I'm proud of you."

Henry grinned as he grabbed the handle of the front door then held it open for her like a little gentleman. Ellie's heart gave a sharp twist. Where had he learned that? It didn't seem like something Jason would have taught him.

"And you're pretty," he added, making Ellie smile.

"Right," she said. "Well, thank you for that. It's just— my job isn't the right kind of job for talking with kids. It's a different kind of job. Does that make sense?"

Henry frowned and shook his head, steering her toward the class. "Are you nervous, Mommy? If you want, we can do lion and fish so your face is ready."

A pang of sadness chattered through her body as Henry led her into the open area between classrooms. Ellie spotted Mrs. Colt in the center of the space and crossed her fingers the teacher would be understanding. Maybe Ellie should focus on explaining things to her before tackling this with Henry.

"Why don't you head on in to class, baby?" She caught Mrs. Colt's eye and waved, then turned back to Henry. "I want to talk with Mrs. Colt alone for just a minute."

"Okay!" He stretched up his arms for a hug, and Ellie bent down to squeeze him tight. She breathed in the scent of baby shampoo and Cinnamon Life and recognized that's what love smelled like.

"Bye, Mommy!" He scurried off toward the classroom, leaving Ellie to face Mrs. Colt alone.

Ellie took a deep breath and turned to the teacher, feeling a bit like a truant pupil. As she approached, Mrs. Colt offered a broad smile. "Good morning!" she sang with a cheer that must be a job requirement for first-grade teachers. "Did you and Henry have a nice weekend?"

"It was great, thanks," Ellie said. She cleared her throat and smoothed down the front of her dress. "Listen, I understand you want to talk about career week. I know Henry volunteered me to speak, but I wanted to explain privately why that might not be such a good idea."

"Oh, dear." Mrs. Colt frowned and glanced toward the classroom.

"I'm so sorry," Ellie said. "I hate to leave you high and dry if you're counting on me, but given what I sell for a living, I thought—"

"No, it's not that," she said. "It's just—well, we already filled your slot."

"Excuse me?" Ellie blinked, wondering if she'd heard right and if "filled your slot" was some sort of Madame Butterfly innuendo. The thought reminded her of the bowling ball conversation with Ty, and she missed him all over again.

"I mean, I guess that's a relief," Ellie continued. "Henry said he volunteered me to speak some time this week, but I didn't realize it was today."

"It wasn't, but we did some shuffling," Mrs. Colt explained. "At the request of Henry's uncle, actually. Since he's on record as Henry's other guardian, I just assumed was acting on your behalf."

"I—we—" Ellie stopped, utterly confused. "Jason? My brother's speaking to the class?"

Mrs. Colt's frown deepened. "Why, no. It's Tyler Hendrix. Your brother said he's a friend of the family?"

Ellie's head began to spin. What on earth was happening? She steadied herself on a bulletin board covered in sheep made with cotton balls and construction paper, too dumbstruck to care that she was crumpling some poor kid's masterpiece.

"Ty," she repeated, her heart speeding up at the sound of his name. "Ty is presenting to the class?"

"Yes," Mrs. Colt said slowly. "Is that okay?"

"It's…it's…unbelievable."

Mrs. Colt gave her an uncertain smile. "He's getting set up right now. Would you like to come in and watch?"

Ellie gave a numb nod and wondered why Jason hadn't mentioned anything. Was this why he'd been so insistent she come in this morning to talk with the teacher?

Mrs. Colt turned toward the classroom, her expression uneasy. "Is this a problem for some reason?" she asked. "I assumed when Jason made the arrangements that—"

"No, it's fine." Ellie forced a smile, as reassuring as she could manage. Her heart was pounding like a jackhammer, and the thought of seeing Ty again made her palms sweaty. "Ty's a great guy. Totally amazing. Smart and talented and—"

*And really, really sexy,* she thought as she stepped through the door and spotted him at the front of the classroom. She froze in the doorway, making Mrs. Colt bump into her from behind. But Ellie hardly noticed. Ty stood there looking rugged and handsome as he watched Henry demonstrate his lion and fish faces.

"Ms. Sanders?"

Ellie turned to see Mrs. Colt giving her an awkward smile and a hand gesture suggesting she move it along.

Right.

Ellie stepped forward in time to see Ty grin down at her kid. All at once, her heart melted into a big, warm puddle of maple syrup.

He looked up then, and Ellie's knees went to goo, too.

Somehow, she remained upright and made her way across the room to an empty chair next to Henry's desk. Seeing her there, Henry said something to Ty then scurried across the room to take his seat.

"Did you see, Mom?" Henry gushed with excitement. "Mr. Ty came. He came to teach the class."

"I see," Ellie said slowly, still not sure what was happening.

"Good morning, boys and girls," Mrs. Colt said, taking her place at the front of the room.

"Good morning, Mrs. Colt," Ellie chorused along with twenty-five small voices.

"This morning we have a very special speaker for career day," she said. "Tyler Hendrix is a partner with Speak Up. It's a video studio that's part of First Impressions Branding & PR. Does anyone know what that means?"

Several hands shot up, including Henry's. Mrs. Colt smiled and deliberately pointed at another little boy on the opposite side of the room. "Joey?"

"Branding is what my grandpa does to his cows," the boy said. "He has a ranch in Montana."

"That's one kind of branding," she said, smiling at Ty before stepping back toward her desk. "I'm actually going to have Mr. Hendrix explain that for us in just a moment. Mr. Hendrix?"

Ty stood up, reminding Ellie all over again what a big man he was. He'd always seemed huge to her, but in a room full of three-foot-tall humans, he looked positively gargantuan.

And positively—*nervous*?

He smiled at her then, trepidation flashing in those

dark brown eyes. She remembered what he'd told her about dreading public presentations. But as he glanced away and directed his gaze over the classroom, he squared his shoulders.

"Good morning," he said with the faintest quiver in his voice. He cleared his throat and continued. "My name is Ty, and I make videos for a living."

"Like for TV?" piped a little girl in the corner.

"Raven," the teacher scolded, giving a stern look. "Remember to raise your hand."

Ty smiled and went on. "Like for TV," he confirmed. "Sometimes it's commercials, and sometimes it's videos like you see on the internet. Who here has watched videos on YouTube?"

A few hands went up, and Ellie said a silent prayer their parents had good monitoring software on their devices. God only knew what kids could see these days. She'd once caught Henry doing a search for "Little Mermaid mating."

Her palms were sweating, and Ellie wiped them on her skirt and tried not to stare at Ty. Then again, he was at the front of a classroom. Wasn't she supposed to stare?

His eyes met hers, and an electric current rattled down her spine. *Those eyes.* They were as dark as she remembered, but there was a light in them now that she hadn't noticed before, some spark that seemed new.

He smiled again and looked back at the students. "Does anyone have any idea how those videos get made?"

A few more hands shot up, but Ty didn't call on anyone this time. Instead, he touched the trackpad of a laptop sitting on the edge of a table beside the whiteboard. The screen behind him flickered to life, and Ty stepped aside, giving everyone a clear view of the presentation.

"I wanted to show you a quick demonstration of how video editing happens," he said. "Henry, would you please turn off the lights?"

Delighted to be called on for a task, Henry scrambled up and flipped the light switch. Hurrying back to his desk, he grinned at Ty, then at Ellie. She reached over and squeezed his hand.

"Good job, baby," she whispered.

"First, I'm going to show you some raw footage from a project I did recently," Ty continued, using a little handheld remote to cue up something from the laptop. "How many of you have been to Great Wolf Lodge?"

Several hands shot up, and two kids in the back of the room began chatting excitedly about the Howlin' Tornado. Ty held up a hand for silence, and the kids obeyed instantly.

"A couple of weeks ago I did a project for them," Ty continued. "Would you like to see some of the video I took from inside the park?"

Ellie found herself nodding, even though it might mean coming face-to-face with photos of herself in a bathing suit. Even as she thought it, she realized Ty wouldn't do that. The man might have faults, but a lack of discretion wasn't one of them.

Amid a chorus of "yes, please," Ty clicked a button on the remote. The screen flashed to life, filled with an image of water crashing from the mouth of River Canyon Run. Then it panned to a shot of the enclosed waterslide tube leading into the pool. From there the footage shifted to the wave pool and a sea of unidentifiable heads and bodies bobbing on the rolling swells. A few more shots of Fort McKenzie followed, with a sweeping shot of the Totem Tower slides, then close-ups of the water jetting from the ground. Ellie's heart gave a soft little hiccup as she remembered how much fun they'd had galloping through the geysers.

Then, the images stopped. Ty surveyed the class and rubbed his hands together. "That's raw footage," he said. "It shows you what the park *looks* like, but not what it *feels* like.

Does anyone know what editing is?"

This time, Henry's hand was the only one that went up. Ty hesitated then pointed to her son. "Henry," he said. "Can you tell me about editing as it relates to videos and not to burping?"

A few kids snickered, and Ellie smiled to herself. Say what you would about Ty Hendrix, but the man was a quick learner.

"It's about looking at the stuff you've got," Henry said. "The good stuff and the bad stuff, and how you make the best out of all of it."

"That's right," Ty said with a note of surprise. Even the teacher appeared impressed, and several kids nodded. Ellie reached over and tousled her son's hair, pleased by his powers of recall. Ty wasn't the only fast learner in the room.

"So now, let me show you an edited version of the footage from that same trip to Great Wolf Lodge." Ty clicked the remote again, toggling to another video file.

Ellie held her breath, not sure what to expect.

Then an image appeared on screen—Henry's face, lit with delight as water droplets glittered on his lashes and he laughed so hard his whole body shook.

Several students shrieked with surprise, and Ellie heard the words *Henry* and *famous* and a lot of others she couldn't make out.

But it was the images on the screen that stole her breath. The camera panned back, sweeping into a dramatic view of the waterslides and pool. Up-tempo music pulsed with the surge of water, and Ellie found herself moving a little to the beat. There was an energy to this footage, something raw and powerful and so filled with happiness it made goose bumps prickle her arms.

The shot cut away again. Another close-up, with her in the frame this time.

But it wasn't the swimsuit-clad shot she'd feared, or even the water park at all. It was a shot of her, bent low over Henry's sleeping form, tucking him into his little bear den bunkbed. His lashes were spread on his cheeks, and as Ellie leaned down to kiss his forehead, she heard a soft murmur of joy from Mrs. Colt.

Or maybe that was Ellie herself. She sat transfixed, savoring this precious moment with her child, treasuring the simple sweetness of it, loving the man who'd captured it.

Then, the scene ended.

The Great Wolf Lodge logo flashed on-screen, but Ellie barely saw it through the sheen of tears in her eyes. Her heart brimmed with gladness and nostalgia and love and so many other things she had no name for.

"That was beautiful," Mrs. Colt whispered.

Ellie nodded and licked her lips, wishing she knew something to say.

"It was just like being there," piped a little girl in the front row.

"That made me happy all over," said the boy beside her.

Voices erupted all over the room, some of them asking Henry what it was like to be famous, while others gushed about how fun the park looked.

As Mrs. Colt shushed them, Ty's eyes locked with Ellie's. Very slowly, he smiled.

"That's editing," he said. "Taking the good stuff and the not-so-good stuff and all the stuff in the middle and making the very best of what you've got."

*That's editing.* Ellie nodded, her gaze still locked with his.

That was more than just editing. That was…that was…

"Magic," she whispered.

Ty smiled wider. "I'm not the best cameraman in the world," he said. "But I do know how to take what I've got and do my very best to make something good. Something meaningful. And I hope that's what each of you gets to do someday for your job."

A few hands shot up in the air, and kids began to pepper Ty with questions about everything from dinosaurs to how many famous people he knew. Most wanted to share rambling stories of their own with little bearing on the lesson he'd just given, but he took it all in stride, responding with patience and grace and a little humor.

Ellie sat watching, amazed by the sight of the man she loved doing the one thing he said he'd never do. Here he was, in front of a room full of kids, being there for her.

For Henry.

As the questions wound down, Mrs. Colt stepped out from behind her desk and got the class's attention. "That's it for our first speaker today, boys and girls. Who's ready to head down to the music room for singing practice?"

A few kids squealed with delight, and several of them began to line up at the door. "Make sure you say thank you to Mr. Hendrix before you go," she called.

"Thank you, Mr. Hendrix!" shouted a sea of cheerful voices as the line began to move toward the door.

"Thank you, Mr. Ty." Henry grinned and ducked past as Ty reached out and tousled his hair.

"Thanks for having me here, little man," Ty said.

"Thank you for coming." Henry looked up and shoved his glasses up his nose. "I missed you."

"I missed you, too, Mr. Henry."

"I've been working on being a gentleman," he said, shifting from one foot to the other. "The good kind."

Ty held out a palm and solemnly shook Henry's hand. "So have I."

Ellie's heart clenched tight in her chest as Henry let go of Ty's hand and scampered out the door with his classmates.

Then, she was alone with Ty.

She stared at him a moment, then unfolded herself from the desk and stood up. "Thank you," she said. "Miriam and my brother must have told you I was in a jam with career day."

"Yes," he said. "But that's not the only reason I came."

Ellie blinked hard, watching his eyes. "Why did you come?"

He reached out and took her hands in his. Electricity arced up her arms and straight to her core. It was the first time he'd touched her since that night he'd said goodbye, and she shivered from the pleasure of it.

"I came to say I'm sorry," he said softly.

"Oh," she said just as softly. "You don't have to—"

"And I came to say I love you, Ellie," he said.

She must have looked stunned, because he squeezed her hands and kept talking, almost like he feared he wouldn't be able to get the words out if he stopped.

"I came because I screwed up, but I'm hoping you can forgive me," he said. "I'm hoping you can give me another chance, and then learn to have patience with me while I figure out how to be a better guy."

Ellie's eyes filled with tears, and she took a deep breath before she answered. "You're already a great guy."

He squeezed her hands again, offering a small, heartfelt smile. "I'm working on it," he said. "But I want to be a better one. For you. And for Henry."

"Ty—"

She didn't know what else to say, and tears clogged her throat, so she settled for nodding like a big, mute moron. Ty smiled and reached up to touch her face.

"Will you forgive me, Ellie?"

"There's nothing to forgive."

"There's plenty to forgive," he said. "There always will be. But I think that figuring out how to do that over and over again is the trick to making it through life."

Ellie's face broke into a smile, and she reached up to touch him. Her fingers traced the stubble on his jaw before sliding down to skim his shoulder, his collarbone, his chest—

Ty flinched. Ellie pulled her hand back, startled. "I'm sorry," she said. "Did I hurt you?"

He shook his head then smiled at her a little sheepishly. "It's just a little tender," he said. "It's still healing."

"What's healing?"

He glanced toward the door, but they were alone, surrounded by empty desks and the minty smell of paint and waxy crayons. Slowly, Ty reached up and undid the first three buttons on his shirt. As he pulled the fabric to the side, Ellie gasped and brought her hands to her mouth.

"Oh my God!" she said. "You covered up Johnny Cash."

Ty nodded and gave another crooked smile.

Ellie stared at the artwork, trying to make sense of it. The skin around it was tender and red, but the image was clear.

*Batman.*

"I found the best cover-up artist in the city," he said. "I'm amazed he managed to do it. If you look right here, you can still see the tip of Johnny's finger behind the edge of the mask."

Ellie stared at it, dumbfounded. "You got a Batman tattoo," she said softly. "For Henry."

"And for me," he murmured, sliding his shirt back into place. "I decided it was time to send the Man in Black packing. To become the Dark Knight instead."

Ellie looked up, tears brimming in her eyes. One spilled down her cheek, and she reached up to link her arms around his neck. "You're already my knight," she said. "My knight in shining armor."

Ty laughed and slid his arms around her waist, pulling her close. Ellie tipped her head back as his lips found hers, certain she'd never been this happy in her life.

# Epilogue

Ty stepped into the waiting room of the hospital birthing center and looked around for a familiar face.

There were quite a few.

But the palest one at the moment belonged to Jason, so Ty made a beeline for Ellie's brother and put a hand on his shoulder.

"Dude, you look like you're going to throw up," he said. "Everything okay?"

Jason shook his head and stood up, looking shaky. "Me? Are you kidding? It's *her* I'm worried about. And the baby."

Ty tried to offer an encouraging smile, but his own nerves and lack of sleep probably made him look like a serial killer.

Miriam stood up and grabbed him by the arm, her one-year-old son propped on one hip. "Come on, Ty! Don't keep us in suspense." She bounced the baby a few times, earning an appreciative glance from Jason, whose eyes dropped quickly to her cleavage.

"Focus," Miriam said, grabbing his chin to direct his attention back to Ty. "Is Ellie okay? And is it a boy or a girl?"

Ty grinned as Henry jumped up on the seat beside them, his head sandwiched between his aunt and uncle's shoulders. He kissed his baby cousin on his downy head, earning a happy gurgle from the baby.

"Am I a brother or a sister?" Henry demanded. "When can I see Mommy?"

"You are definitely a brother," Ty told him. "And if you're ready to meet your baby sister, we can go back there right now. Would you like that?"

Henry beamed and nodded, while a collective wave of relief washed over the whole room. "You go first, buddy," Jason said. "We don't want to freak her out with all of us storming in there like demons."

"Good call." Miriam bounced the baby again, then bent to plant a kiss on his dimpled cheek. "I remember how overwhelming those first few hours felt."

"Hours?" Jason laughed. "Try months."

The waiting room doors swished open, and Holly Colvin rushed in, smiling at everyone. Miriam and Ty's business partner hustled over to them and pressed a gift bag into his hands. "I hope I'm not too late," she said. "Sorry I can't stay. Ben's at home on potty-training duty with Evan, but I wanted to congratulate you and see how everything turned out."

"We had a little girl," Ty said, his chest swelling at the words. "A daughter. She's beautiful, just like her mom."

Holly beamed and squeezed Ty's hand. "I'm so happy for you."

"Thank you." Ty clutched the gift bag to his chest as a wave of gratitude washed through him. "Maybe when we're home later this week we can have you over for dinner."

Holly and Miriam exchanged a glance then burst into laughter. Jason reached out and clapped him on the shoulder.

"Buddy," he said. "You've got a lot to learn."

Miriam grinned and bounced the baby some more.

"Spoken like a man who's never eaten uncooked ramen noodles straight from the pouch after six sleepless nights of midnight feedings."

"Or gone to work with spit-up on his shirt," Jason added.

"Or put his phone in the microwave instead of a bottle of formula," Holly added, grinning.

"I'm looking forward to all of it," Ty said, surprised to realize he sort of was. Okay, so he was anxious and a little freaked out, and he knew there were a zillion ways to screw up these kids. But at the moment, as he looked down at Henry, the main thing he felt was love.

"Come on, buddy," he said, tousling his stepson's hair. "Want to meet your baby sister?"

Henry nodded and held out his hand. Ty took it, and together they walked back to the alcove where Ty showed him how to scrub his hands well. Then they walked side by side to the birthing suite where Ellie lay cradling an infant in her arms. She looked up as they walked in, and beamed.

"My favorite boys," she said, angling the bundle to show them. "Want to meet her?"

Henry nodded and stepped forward, his little face filled with awe. He peered down at the pink bundle, poking his glasses up on his nose. "Do you know what her name is?"

Ty bit back a laugh, charmed by the idea that the baby might have emerged with a business card announcing her name and job title.

"Lily," Ellie said. "She's named after my mother."

"And her middle name is Renee," Ty said. "For my grandmother."

Ellie smiled up at him, and Ty was certain his heart would burst with pride. "I texted with your sister a few seconds ago," she said. "She'll be here in an hour."

Ty nodded, overwhelmed with joy that his wife and sister had bonded so well. "She stopped to visit John—um, our father."

*Our father.*

The word sounded odd, and he thought of Johnny back behind bars again. The image was nothing at all like the father Ty wanted to be.

But he was working on forgiveness. It came easier for Anna, but Ty was trying. While he'd never forget the way his father abandoned him, forgiveness did seem like something he could manage eventually. Ellie and Henry and now Lily— they'd made it possible.

"Here," Ellie said, angling up in the bed to hold out the baby. "Let's let Daddy hold her for a minute. And if he sits over there in that chair, I can grab a picture of the three of you together."

Ty leaned down and picked up his daughter, marveling at the weight of her—at the fact that he was holding a tiny human being that he'd helped create.

He made his way over to the easy chair across from the bed and sat down. Henry followed then wriggled into the crook of Ty's opposite arm. As the boy cuddled against his chest, Ty took a deep breath.

He looked down at his kids—*his kids*—and an explosion of love knocked him back in the chair. Tears of happiness pricked the back of his eyelids, and he gazed at Ellie to see her eyes glittering, too.

She held up her iPhone camera, tilting it to the side as she tried to get the right angle. "Okay, you guys," she said. "Say cheese."

"Cheeeese!" Henry said, tilting his chin up the way he always did in family photos. His glasses were crooked, and there was a faint hint of grape Popsicle around his mouth. Ty glanced at his own shirt, realizing he'd already managed to amass a bit of baby slobber on his collar.

Ellie looked down at her iPhone, thumb sliding over the screen as she scrolled through the pictures. "We might have to do a retake later," she said, tucking a strand of blond hair behind one ear as she met Ty's eyes again. "Maybe when everyone's cleaned up and looking their best."

Ty shook his head and gazed down at his daughter, smiling as she made a face he suspected had something to do with poop.

"No," he said, shifting a little to let Henry snuggle closer against his chest. The boy peered at his baby sister while Ty looked up at his wife and grinned. "It's perfect already. No editing required."

# Acknowledgments

I'm eternally grateful to fans of the First Impressions series who've read the previous two books voraciously enough to land the first one on the USA Today bestseller list. You guys are what keeps me writing on days I think it might be easier to give up the author gig and become a professional sasquatch hunter.

So much love and thanks to my critique partners and beta readers, including Linda Grimes, Kait Nolan, and Cynthia Reese. I'm also super-grateful to my assistant (aka Wonder Girl Ass) Meah Cukrov for all your work keeping me organized and on track.

Though I already dedicated this book to Fenske's Frisky Posse, I'd be remiss if I didn't mention my awesome street team again because you guys rock so hard you make me seasick. Thank you for talking up my books, leaving reviews, and generally making me feel like a rock star (minus the cocaine habit and pink hair).

Huge thanks to Liz Pelletier of Entangled Publishing for taking me from, "Meh, I like this book just fine," to

"OHMYGOD I can't wait for everyone to read it!" You've done so much to fine-tune my writing, and I'm excited for our next project together. Thanks also to Jessica Turner, Melanie Smith, Heather Riccio, Christine Chhun, Bridget O'Tooole, and anyone else on the Entangled team who I might have inadvertently forgotten here. Love you guys!

As always, I'm so thankful to have Michelle Wolfson of Wolfson Literary Agency on my team (and I'm grateful it's not a basketball team, since we'd both suck at that). Thanks for keeping my career on track and being my number one advocate and partner.

Thank you to my stepkids, Cedar and Violet, for doing all kinds of adorable stuff to inspire the things that come out of Henry's mouth in this story. You guys are the best!

I owe an extra-big debt of gratitude to my husband, Craig Zagurski, for not only inspiring a video producer hero, but for all your tireless work on promotional content for all my books. I'm so glad we're in this together, hot stuff. Love you!

# About the Author

Tawna Fenske traveled a career path that took her from newspaper reporter to English teacher in Venezuela to marketing geek to PR manager for her city's tourism bureau. An avid globetrotter and social media fiend, Tawna is the author of the popular blog, Don't Pet Me, I'm Writing, and a member of Romance Writers of America. She lives with her husband in Bend, Oregon, where she'll invent any excuse to hike, bike, snowshoe, float the river, or sip wine on her back deck. She's published several romantic comedies with Sourcebooks, including *Making Waves*, which was nominated for contemporary romance of the year by RT Book Reviews. She also writes heartwarming series books for Entangled Publishing, and tender, funny romances for Montlake Publishing. Tawna's quirky brand of comedy and romance has won praises from Kirkus Reviews, which noted, "Up-and-coming romance author Fenske sets up impeccable internal and external conflict and sizzling sexual tension for a poignant love story between two engaging characters, then infuses it with witty dialogue and lively humor. An appealing blend of lighthearted fun and emotional tenderness."

*Find love in unexpected places with these satisfying Lovestruck reads...*

## A Taste of You
### a *Bourbon Boys* novel by Teri Anne Stanley

Good thing Eve likes a challenge. That's exactly what she'll face trying to convince a flaky contractor's hunky son to tackle the distillery's visitor center so she can cross another item off her very organized to-do list. Commitment-phobe carpenter Nick Baker can't resist helping sexy Eve out of her jam. But, her addictive, forever-flavored kisses push him out of his caution zone, and if he's not careful his past will nail him to the wall.

## Catching the Cowgirl
### a *Cotton Creek* novel by Jennie Marts

When California video game designer Adam Clark comes to a Colorado dude ranch to research his latest game, he figures his biggest challenge will be lasting the week. Then he meets the ranch's owner, cowgirl Skye Hawkins...and suddenly, one week isn't anywhere near long enough.

## The Right Ranger
### a *Men of At Ease Ranch* novel by Donna Michaels

Former Army Ranger Cord Brannigan secretly promised his fallen teammate he'd protect the tempting, fiercely independent Haley Wagner from a distance, but now they're stuck together for three weeks. Alone. Keeping his hands *off* will take every ounce of control he can muster. And that control is slipping...

67185683R00145